The Love
He Left Behind

Mary Jean Kelso

Published in the United States of America
MarKel Press, P.O. Box 362, Fernley, NV 89408
MJKel@aol.com
maryjeankelsoauthor.wix.com/mjkel
Copyright © January 2016 Mary Jean Kelso
All rights reserved.
ISBN: 0-9621406-5-1
ISBN-13: 978-0-9621406-5-5

DEDICATION

To all of you who have experienced a First Love —
Know that there will be residual effects that form your destiny,
good or bad.
Nobody forgets their First Love.

Cover Design by Wendy Whiteman

ACKNOWLEDGMENTS

Thanks to Linda Rettstatt for her major assistance and technical help in formatting this book.
Thanks to my niece, Amy Brush, who agreed to be the First Reader for THE LOVE HE LEFT BEHIND.

CHAPTER ONE

A lone rider sat astride his horse on a rise above a small Indian settlement near Pyramid Lake, Nevada. What was he, a wanted man, doing in a Godforsaken place so recent to death and destruction?

To his left at a distance, light glowed dimly from a window in a homesteader's cabin. The greased paper covering the hole cut into a wall lit up only the misshapen square. It warned the rider watching the abode that the inhabitants had not yet retired at this late hour.

Whether warranted, or not, the rider sensed danger from a vigilant settler. While the darkness of night hid him from any resident or native that might look his way his horse twitched nervously, sensing his master's uneasiness.

The rider knew, not many years before, the Paiutes fought the United States Cavalry near this point. Now there were only the flickers of dying campfire flames illuminating through slits in the Indians' reed- and scrap-constructed shelters in the area below far to the right from the homesteader's cabin.

Many lives were lost, including that of Captain Storey

3

who was taken back to Virginia City for burial once the skirmish was over.

The Paiute Chief, Numaga, warned his council that fighting a war with the encroaching settlers would bring so many of their enemy to battle that they would outnumber the Paiutes, "like sand in a whirlwind." He chose not to fight. To live in peace. A massacre at Williams Station in retaliation for the kidnapping and enslavement of Indian girls brought the council to an end. The Indians knew there would be no chance to avoid a war. The heavily-armed cavalry and volunteers were sure to drive the Paiutes from their land. Many, on both sides, died in an attempt of the Paiutes to hold onto one tiny piece of what they deemed to be their homeland. Their very survival depended on it.

For all the passerby, Clay Bingham, knew many bodies might lay buried beneath his horse's hooves where they now stood. The ground might well be saturated with the blood of the white man and his enemy. Yet, there he sat in his saddle, staring down on a dimly lit cabin constructed, now, not far from the battlefield and the current Indian encampment.

Times were changing. A marker he had rode past designated the Pyramid Lake Paiute Tribes' Reservation. Neighbors to the reservation, the homesteaders lived and minded their own business over the invisible lines designating where Indian land and the homesteaders claims began. Natives and settlers survived without fear of retribution — as long as no one intruded on the other.

A snow squall whipped thick white flakes around Clay's shoulders and onto his heavily bearded face. Snow he understood from past experience to be created by a cold wind blowing off Pyramid Lake. It swirled, sticking to the faded, threadbare serape he wore for more warmth over his thick wool coat.

Bad weather! He had spent two miserable winters and three exceptionally hot summers herding cattle in Montana while trying to outrun the accusations and threats from people in his former hometown near here.

Those years working on a Montana ranch hadn't made him like dreadful conditions any better than he ever did. What else could he expect? Who would follow their heart's folly on a quest for the woman he loved in such conditions? He considered the fact that he might be mad. Might well have lost his mind while trying to save his body these last few years.

Since it was snowing this hard here, he imagined further south the high altitude trail around Lake Tahoe was impassable. Most of the Donner Party perished some time back when they tried to make the crossing late in the year. An unexpected storm blew in and trapped them in the high Sierra Mountains one winter. Few survived, and those that did, lived by resorting to cannibalism. *Could his foolish heart lead him into destruction as well?*

"Damn!" He spoke aloud to his horse, Buckshot, "What I wouldn't give for a hot cup of coffee for me and a warm stable for you to bed down in."

Buckshot, a strong bay gelding not nearly as beautiful as the buckskin, Adonis, he'd owned before, snorted at snowflakes that landed on his nose. He shook his head to toss them off and faced away from the storm as best he could. The wind ahead of the incoming storm blew his tail tight against his body as he tried to position himself against the onslaught. He pawed the ground with his right fore foot as if he could remove the snow that began to rapidly accumulate. Buckshot, having been a wrangler's mount for Clay in Montana, and most of Clay's parting pay, was no stranger to snow. He was familiar enough with it to want to move on and get out of the snowstorm.

Once he seemed settled into position to ward off the weather, Clay reined him in place as he studied the deteriorating situation.

It could be only a squall that would diminish as he rode south along the trail toward Wadsworth, he considered. Further from the lake the moisture might turn to rain or stop entirely in that direction. *But, would it?* He knew he couldn't count on it.

Clay thought about what had led him back here in the first place. It had been his home, once. He knew the land nearby well.

His parents homesteaded 160 acres a few miles to the southeast along the Carson River. There, the Indians thought of them as encroachers on land they had considered theirs since all eternity.

It was a place that would be his now, if the taxes hadn't eaten it up. He wondered, *could he ever go back again, anyway, to what he had once called home?*

~*~

As painful as it was, he remembered how the day that changed his life forever started out. It was like any other on the homestead that spring many years ago

He was a young boy then, small enough to ride a pony bareback, but on the verge of outgrowing even that.

"Clay, get down off Scamper and put him in the corral and do your chores," his Pa called.

He did as he was told, begrudging the fact that he would have to forego an early morning ride to his favorite spot on the Bingham land. It was an area by the water that ran from the Carson River and pooled into a miniature lake where tall reeds grew along its edge.

"Yes, Pa," he answered and opened the corral gate to let Scamper inside for food and water.

He walked toward where his father worked under shade

from a roof erected near the barn. His Pa hammered a piece of hot metal on an anvil. He pounded it steadily into a part he needed to repair the rusty plow that threatened to deteriorate before the ground was turned for the family's vegetable garden.

Clay, a boy of eight, then, tended to his own chores inside the barn while he looked forward to mounting onto Scamper's back later for a ride to his secret hiding place.

He knew his Ma was busily cleaning up the breakfast dishes. She prepared to heat the water he carried earlier by buckets for the chore.

He, nor his Pa, heard them coming.

They slipped silently into the yard, as they had done so many times before. They stood at the door of the cabin waiting for his Ma to offer them food. These stragglers of starving Indians, that had little left once they were forced onto the reservation, normally came as peaceful beggars.

As if sensing a difference in these unwelcome visitors, his Pa stopped hammering and looked up toward the house.

"Clay, them pesky Indians are back," he called to him.

Clay looked through a crack in the barn. They were hungry, he knew. But these were different Indians. Not the ones that were known to him that strayed in off nearby rangeland that barely supported wild mustangs much less humans.

His Pa laid the part he worked on beside the anvil and moved toward the house with his hammer still in one big hand and his rifle in the other.

"Here! You go on. We got nothing to spare today," Clay heard his father call out.

The Indians looked at him.

"I said, go on."

At the sound of his voice, Clay's Ma opened the door on the cabin. She stood speechless confronted by three of the

7

four hungry renegades.

The fourth turned and walked toward his Pa. Before his Pa could raise his rifle, the Indian jumped him, wrestling him to the ground.

The rifle fired. Clay waited for his Pa to get up and take aim at the other Indians, who now shoved his Ma back into the cabin. But, his Pa lay flat on the dirt in the yard. He didn't move.

The Indian stepped away from his Pa. He took the rifle and entered the house behind the others.

Clay wanted to call to his Pa. But, fright held his tongue still.

He heard the rifle fire again and he dropped to the barn floor and crawled out a loose board in the back of the building. He ran toward the trees along the Carson River. He hid there while he watched the Indians leave the cabin taking what they could carry with them, including his Pa's rifle. They mounted bareback on the horses in the corral and rode off leading Scamper behind them.

Clay did what his parents had instructed him to do, living in this hard land.

"Get away and stay away if there's trouble. Don't come back, no matter what," his Pa's words echoed in his brain. "Go for help as soon as you can."

Clay lay snug in the cradle of a large cottonwood tree's roots where the river had washed the soil away during a flood. He squeezed his eyes tight, not wanting to see the horror before him. He choked back tears for his parents and Scamper.

At last he heard multiple horses racing toward him above the noise of the high-running stream. The runoff of water from heavy winter snows in the mountains lapped the soft bank below his feet. A large chunk of sandy loam dropped into the fast moving water with a loud splash. The noise startled him. His eyes popped open and he jumped, staring into the stream expecting to see an Indian standing there. He watched with relief as the clump of dirt dissolved as the river carried it away.

Still, he hid.

The sound of the hooves became louder. He smelled smoke in the air.

The Indians had been on foot until they took the family's few horses. *Had they known how many people lived on the homestead? Were they searching for him now? Had they set fire to the brush to flush him out? Surely, they would be riding slower if they were following his tracks,* he considered. He hoped they hadn't known he was in the barn when they attacked.

As he listened to the sound of the hooves coming closer he heard a man's voice shout.

"They've set fire to the Bingham place!"

"Wasn't the massacre at Williams Station enough? I thought we settled this thing years ago," another voice reached him.

"We took care of that bunch of renegades back then. This must be some other band," the first voice, closer now, answered.

Realizing the words were those he understood and not that of the Native tongue, Clay darted out toward the sound of the approaching riders.

He saw that, although they rode like Cavalry, they were dressed in civilian clothes. *Could it be a posse?*

Several men reined their mounts to a stop when they saw him. One of them motioned for the others to continue on.

"I'll be right on your heels. Don't let 'em get away."

"Help me. That's my Ma and Pa over there," Clay pleaded.

The lead man reached his hand down to hoist Clay up behind him.

"Hang on. When we get close, I'll drop you somewhere that you can hide nearby. Stay away from the house, you understand? I'll take you back to safety while the rest of the men track those renegades down."

Clay never returned to the yard of the homestead where his Pa lay. Captain Collier, as Clay soon learned was his rescuer's name, hesitated at a clump of sagebrush near the corner of the barn where Clay had escaped.

"Stay put! I'll be back for you. Stay as close as you can between the barn and the brush," he instructed the frightened boy. "Don't move!" Captain Collier called back over his shoulder as he spurred his white steed on toward the house some yards away from the barn.

Clay saw the source of the smoke and felt a sickness in his stomach. Flames shot from the side of the cabin where the cook-stove's metal pipe lay on the ground instead of keeping what was a utilitarian fire controlled. No doubt the inside of what he had called home was wrecked and, probably, on fire. He wondered about his Ma, fearing the second shot he heard had been for her.

No, no. Don't even think that, he pleaded with his mind. But, even as he tried to deny what might be the truth, he felt the outcome for his Ma would not be good.

Clay saw the men hesitate in the front yard. One man dropped to the ground and leaned over his Pa's body. Another edged his mount up onto the front porch and rode halfway through the open front door. Then, he turned to the man that appeared to be in command and shook his head.

The man called back to him, "Smith, you're in charge now. Take the men on and cut the renegades off before they kill more settlers. I'm going to take the boy back myself. I'll round up more men to help you. Whatever you do, don't lose their trail!"

The man, who had lifted him onto the horse before, rode toward him again. Clay raised up from the ground to his feet behind the sagebrush and stood waiting for word about his parents.

The man reined the large white horse to a stop in front of him. It shook its head, whipping its long mane back and forth as it pawed the dirt as though eager to get on with its run.

Clay looked at the rider. Questions swirled in his mind.

The man studied the boy for a moment.

"I'm Captain Collier. Leastwise, that's what I was called in the Civil War. Sure sorry to tell you, boy, but they're both gone."

"Clay," the word stumbled off his tongue. "Clay Bingham." Clay responded feeling a sense of total collapse inside and wondering at his own reality amidst this unreal situation.

"If you had any animals over there, boy, looks like they took off with them, too. Climb back up here," the Captain kicked his foot free from his left stirrup so Clay could use it to heft himself back up behind the saddle.

"I saw them take the horses," Clay said. He was sure he would never see Scamper again.

"The boys will come back and take care of your folks. No point in you going over there now. We'll find some place for you to stay at my ranch. Hang on tight. I gotta get them boys some more help."

The Captain kicked his horse in the flanks with both boot heels and raced toward the nearest settlement.

Clay clung to the Captain's heavy jacket and felt the stride of the mighty animal as the Captain raced them back to civilization. Every jar of hoof against the trail brought tears from Clay's eyes and he fought to keep them away.

His parents were gone. He was too young to be on his own. He had no other family to care for him and he was sure he couldn't manage the homestead alone. It was his parent's dream to build a home for all of them and now, they were gone along with all their dreams.

What was an eight-year-old boy to do? His heart ached. He could not believe his Pa and Ma were alive one second and dead the next. Everything he knew was gone, or soon would be, destroyed in the fire. *What could he do? He was helpless.* As bad as he wanted to turn back to the time before the crack of his father's rifle, he knew he couldn't undo what had been done. He sensed a profound loss and every beat of the horse's hooves taking him away from the homestead took him into a deeper shock of disbelief.

~*~

Survive, Clay thought now as he stared, as a grown man, into the snowstorm toward the Indian encampment. *They were living in peace today. Even then, the other Indians could not have been blamed for what a small group of renegades did,* he told himself. *Wars started when you did that.*

As his mind traveled back to his transition from the homestead to the Collier Ranch, he remembered Captain Collier made no demands on him. He simply moved him into his house with him and his wife, Maggie.

Their vast spread supported a large herd of cattle and a string of quarter horses bred to work them. Profits from the sale of the livestock also supported cowboys and their families. *What was one more mouth to feed?*

Captain Collier saw that Clay had what he needed and watched him grow.

Early on, the Captain introduced Clay to a buckskin gelding named after the Greek God, Adonis. Adonis ran as fast as the wind of a Washoe Zephyr. He could beat nearly any cowboy's steed in cutting cattle from the herd. He was quick on his feet whether galloping over the ground or doing fancy footwork on the job. His steps were like a dandy dancing from a ruffian's bullets.

Clay remembered the rides atop Adonis with the Captain along side on his great white horse. Not only he and Adonis grew closer, but he and the Captain did as well. Captain Collier became his mentor and taught him things that would have been his Pa's place to see that he learned.

When the nightmares came in the dark, and he broke into a sweat reliving the horror, it was always the Captain who came to comfort him.

Later, he sensed the Captain was outside the door of the small bedroom, pacing in his bare feet on the cold floor until Clay slept soundly again. The man searched for a way to help Clay forget — or, at least a way to ease his pain.

As Clay became older and accepted the heavy lead ball of dread that hung in his heart like a clock pendulum, he deemed he would, one day, pay back Captain Collier for caring for him all those many years. At sixteen, Clay moved into the bunkhouse and demanded to do his part in running the ranch.

"Only if you let me pay you the same as any other ranch hand," Captain Collier insisted.

"But, you've already done so much."

"You pulled your own weight as you were growing up. We'll call it even and start over. If you want to be a wrangler, you'll get paid as one. Fair enough?"

Clay nodded. He didn't want to take more than his room and board. But, he knew Captain Collier wouldn't hear of anything else except a fair wage for a fair day's work.

~*~

Now, as the snow swirled around him, it seemed as if that were another life eons ago. He set his sights on what

13

once was home territory a few miles ahead where the small settlement of early pioneers had built a town.

It had been a long time ago that the Indians fought the Cavalry at Pyramid Lake and, in the end, moved to reservations.

He knew the old homestead where he left his childhood behind was within fifty miles of where he sat his mount as a man. As was Captain Collier's ranch. But, for Clay, this was, now, unfriendly territory. The sooner he did what he came to do and got on down the road, the better. Clay decided, once he got through Wadsworth, a small railroad town, he'd turn east for a ways before going south and working his way to Tonopah avoiding crossing the Sierras.

It was nearing Christmas and winter held a tight grasp on this part of the country in December.

He didn't want to deal with any more nasty weather conditions than necessary.

It had been years since he left the growing settlement in a hurry. His exodus had not been his idea.

CHAPTER TWO

If the truth be known, a group of angry men ran him out of the rough and tumble community.

Now, as he let his eyes follow the dim outlines of the buildings lit in the glow of a lantern here and there, he noted that an occasional house window shown with small flickering candles positioned on Pinion tree branches that supported the candle bases.

It had been a long time since he celebrated the warmth of the holiday. Once he left the area, he saw no reason to participate in celebrations of any kind.

Slowly, Clay moved Buckshot ahead. They came off a low ridge and into the valley. True to his earlier comment to Buckshot, he thought the animal would probably appreciate getting out of the weather as much as he would. He moved through what wasn't much more than a whistle-stop at Wadsworth and aimed straight for the next cluster of buildings that sat at Wadsworth's back door only a short distance away. There, he hoped to find a saloon.

He had, at first, considered skirting this area as well. But, he knew it was another thirty or so miles on east to

Ragtown where emigrants came to the Carson River after surviving their trek across the Forty Mile Desert.

Horse and rider wanted out of the inclement conditions and, even though the next settlement was where he ran into trouble a few years back, it was a place he favored for several reasons.

He walked Buckshot past the train cars sitting on a siding outside of Wadsworth. Their wooden skeletons appeared like apparitions in the dim reflection of snow as their wheels wrapped their rims on the metal rails.

He heard a clatter and a drifter dropped out of a cattle car and ran from the open door.

Clay, probably as startled as the man had been at his approach, turned Buckshot quickly to the side and moved away from the tracks.

He took a different path toward the buildings he knew would be clustered a bit farther on. Remembering the route the immigrants took to get to California, he eased Buckshot onto the widened stretch through the sandy swales.

There, wagon trains had cut deep ruts between the settlements and what was now the Reservation. Nothing inhabited this part of the desert terrain except rattlesnakes, lizards and scorpions. In the cold he wasn't worried about the natural, if hazardous, animals being out. No housing or businesses were within a couple of miles. Here he could approach the area from the northeast end instead of the more heavily traveled west side.

As he rode he made plans on how he would avoid a run-in with the locals. He hoped no one recognized him. Arriving late at night had been in his plans for that very reason. Fewer people moving about raised his odds of not being seen by a long-time resident.

It was dangerous ground he was on now and he knew it was foolish to be there. But, his desire to find out if the life he left behind could be the same again tugged heavily at his heart and swayed his common sense. He told himself he wouldn't have to mingle with the general population in the daylight.

With any luck, no one would know him, now. He could warm himself, have a meal and a good night's rest, then be on his way tomorrow. Christmas Eve.

Remembering the holiday, he cringed as his mind finally admitted the real reason he was returning to his home place. He thought about Holly O'Flannery.

She was probably married to someone else by now. She most likely had forgotten him or, at least tried to, and gone on with her life. After all, no one could expect a woman to wait for a man who would ride out on her with no explanation or any sort of goodbye. He understood that.

Chances were she wasn't even living here any longer. And, he didn't care, he tried to tell himself. But deep down inside, he felt a stir in his heart as he remembered the last Christmas Eve they spent together.

~*~

As he neared the structures clustered ahead, he recalled that night when he was with her in this little colony far off the main path to anywhere situated between the Truckee Meadows and points east. Holly had always been the draw for his visits to the community.

Silently, he cursed his heart's folly and wished he could forget Holly. But his mind went back to what he considered his last Christmas. For, without Holly, there was no reason to celebrate.

What did he think, by coming here he could recapture the sense he had felt when he could reach out and touch her? When life, for him, was real and love was what seemed, now, all too brief?

At first, when he was a child, it seemed his life ended

when his parents were killed. Then, again when Captain Collier was murdered and he was blamed for the crime. *How many lives did he think he had?* He wondered as his mind replayed happier times. If nine, like a cat, he'd already used up too many of them.

~*~

The last time Holly O'Flannery saw Clay she had barely finished crocheting the second mitten of a set for her little sister, Amy. She prepared to crochet the yarn into a long strand to attach one end to each of the two hand warmers. By creating a connecting string to both she thought the child would be less likely to lose either of them when they were tugged over her fingers and her arms thrust down the sleeves of her heavy coat.

There was a knock at the door and Holly put her work down next to the matching mitten.

She rose to lift the flour-sack curtain aside and look out the one small window. It was situated on the front of the clapboard cabin her father built before her mother died. As small as the single pane was, it gave her a view of anyone close outside.

Clay stood back and waved toward the window to let her know it was he who called.

Her younger siblings, two-year-old Amy and five-year-old Bradley, slept on their heavy pads in the loft overhead. She hurried to open the door and quiet him before either of them awoke from the noise of his knock or the creak of the door.

"It's me, Clay," a low voice told her through a slight crack between the door and its casing.

"Yes. I know." Her heart was already racing at the glimpse of him she had seen while he stood in the cold waiting for her to answer his knock.

She lifted the heavy board that secured the family safe

inside their home from intruders, from its metal brackets.

Holly, a tiny Irish girl, fought back her excitement at his unexpected appearance. Her pale blue eyes took in his discomfort with the weather as she tried to keep a poker face that belied her joy.

She had the brightest unruly red hair Clay Bingham had ever seen. He took in her features as she gently eased the door open to avoid as many squeaks as possible.

Clay hadn't known many women, or girls for that matter, in his secluded life on the ranch. Still, of the few he had, he thought Holly was the prettiest girl he ever set eyes on.

Her rush and concern to let him enter as quickly and quietly as possible flushed her cheeks. The rosy tint only added to her beauty.

Clay stood inside taking in her vision with the flickering light from the fireplace glowing around her.

He nearly gasped as he thought about the first time he saw her. He knew he would never find another girl like her.

~*~

Clay had been wrangling stray calves out of the brambles down near a creek on Captain Collier's ranch one day when he came upon what he thought was a young child.

"Oh!" Holly had shrieked in surprise when he broke through the heavy sagebrush. He emerged from a thicket where she was picking berries on a rare cascade of greenery.

Startled as well, Clay quickly removed his hat and held it over his chest to let her know he meant no harm. He ran his fingers through his hair and regretted the rips the brambles had made in his shirt and pants.

"I — I — thought you were a bear!" The girl exclaimed.

Clay saw panic registered on her face.

Now that she saw she was not in line for a fierce animal attack, she still gathered her skirts to run.

19

She turned and sprinted away on bare feet, spilling berries in a trail on the ground behind her.

"Wait!" Clay called after her as she hurried to her straggly mule nearby.

Before he could stop her, she climbed atop a canvas-wrapped pile of prospector's tools.

Clay took another step forward.

"Stop!" She held her hand up, palm out.

She grabbed the mule's reins and tried to kick the beast in the sides to start him forward.

Clay did as he was told. Still in shock at finding a girl on the other side of the brush, he looked at her as if she were a ghost.

"Don't come after me, if you know what's good for you. My Pa's just down the creek a ways mining. He's got a gun, so it would be best if you stayed away."

Finally the mule obeyed her command and lumbered its way along the trail worn close to the bank of the creek.

Clay stood looking after her.

"My God! Where did she come from?" He asked himself aloud. He knew in that moment he would have to find out. For now, he wouldn't follow her. But, he thought, there had to be some way to meet her where she would feel safe and it would be acceptable.

~*~

Her words shook him from his reverie.

"Clay, what are you doing here so late?" Holly asked as he squeezed past her with his arms loaded with firewood from the stack on the porch.

"I was coming to town and thought I'd stop and see if you wanted company," he said as he knelt to relieve his arms of their burden. He placed two sticks of wood in the fireplace flames. Smoke from the burning wood seeped into the room with a sweet smell. The glow the fire made cast

20

bright shimmers of light throughout the small drab room. It cheered the normally dull bare wooden walls making the room appear pleasant and peaceful in the fire's glow.

He wished he had a large oak log, like they had back at the Collier Ranch, to put onto the fire. That would keep Holly and her charges warm throughout the night. He knew the small pieces of split cottonwood from the porch would burn quickly. In the raw cold of morning, Holly would get up to find dead coals in the fireplace and shiver while she rekindled the previous night's fire.

"If my Pa finds you here, there'll be trouble," Holly warned, jarring him from his momentary reverie.

"I don't think he'll know," Clay said. Not explaining that he had already seen Ian O'Flannery stumbling from one saloon tent in the roadway to another on the opposite side where more half tent, half boards formed a refuge for tired miners and cowboys.

Most nights Holly's Pa, a hardscrabble miner that scavenged played-out spots on someone else's claim when they moved on, spent his time easing his pain in the saloons until well after midnight. Like a good many miners, he was also a hard drinker when he wasn't working a claim somewhere. And, usually, even when he was.

"It's Christmas Eve. Bradley and Amy are already asleep. They're anticipating presents in the morning. I still have a few stitches to make so there'll be something under the tree for them," Holly explained. She looked at the scraggly Pinion pine standing in the corner of the room with popcorn strung on strings woven through its branches. It was pitiful and, she knew, it would soon be cut into pieces and fed to the fire when its purpose was served.

"About that," Clay said and pulled a paper bag from his coat pocket. "I got paid today. It isn't much but I brought some hard candy and an orange for each of you, if you'd like to see that the kids get them in the morning."

"Clay, how sweet of you! Yes. They'll love it. And I will, too." She took the bag to hide it until later when she would fill each child's stocking before she went to bed. For fun, she decided she would put one of her stockings up and drop her orange in that as well.

She had seen oranges, a rare treat, at the General Store earlier. And, she had stood smelling the tangy aroma and marveling at the fruit in the small basket. The container was already half empty. She knew they would soon be gone but her few coins her father had left her on his way out that morning were not enough to purchase anything more than absolute necessities.

It pained her to have the children ask for the treats when she couldn't get them what they wanted. She was happy they would have something special Christmas morning.

The O'Flannery family didn't have much, Clay knew. Nor did he. But then, he managed on his own with no family to worry about since Captain Collier rescued him as a boy. When he finished his day's labor at the ranch there was always a hot meal and a dry bunk waiting for him.

What the heck, as much as he appreciated what the Colliers did for him, he didn't have anyone to spend his money on for Christmas anyway. The Colliers wouldn't hear of him buying them presents. He didn't drink, so there really wasn't much he needed. At least, not much that took money to get. A good ride on Adonis suited him just fine.

He waited until Holly came back to the fireplace where he stood warming his hands. She moved close beside him.

"One more thing — or two," he said and reached his hand into the open front of the coat he still wore. He pulled a small rag doll and a wooden whistle from inside. He showed them to Holly.

"The whistle sounds like a steam train," he explained to her as he kneeled to put both beneath the pathetic tree.

"There, that looks better."

Holly had tears in her eyes.

"Yes. Much better," she agreed.

Neither spoke for a moment.

Unsure of himself, Clay lifted one of her heavy red curls with his forefinger and studied the tight coil in the firelight.

She turned her face toward him and gazed into his eyes.

The flickering light softened the tone of her skin until she appeared like an angel in its muted glow.

"To tell the truth I'd already settled into my bunk tonight. I got to thinking about how we met."

Holly giggled softly.

"I don't know, now, who scared whom the worse." Her lips curved into a sweet smile.

"Darn right! I was set to throw a lasso over a calf and there was this — this — lovely creature — standing there!"

Clay took her hand in his, weaving their fingers together much like she crocheted her yarn.

"And, I don't know which scared me the most. Thinking you were a bear or finding that you were a man — maybe a desperado."

"Guess we'll always remember that day," Clay said and raised her hand to his lips. He looked into her eyes as though asking permission before kissing each small knuckle.

"Clay —," she said hesitantly.

"Are you afraid of me, still? Do you want me to leave now?" Clay asked.

"No. But I am afraid of what will happen If my Pa comes home."

"Don't worry. He won't be here for awhile," he assured her. He leaned his face toward hers and tilted her chin up to kiss her lips.

23

"Clay," she whispered. "You know I can't."

"Can't what?" he asked as his lips brushed hers tenderly.

"I can't do these things. I have the other kids to think about. How would they survive without me to look after them?"

"It's not like I'm asking you to run away, Holly. We can stay right here. I heard some of the men are building a schoolhouse a few blocks away. You can still help your family. All I'm asking is that you marry me. Some day we'll have a family of our own."

Holly felt the heat of his lips on hers and let herself be caught up in his embrace.

She loved him more than he knew. She had anticipated his arrival this evening without even knowing he was coming. In that hope, she had heated the curling iron in the coals earlier in the evening and twisted her hair into the long ringlets she knew he liked.

She was only a couple of years younger than Clay. She was mature for her age, from caring for the younger children in the family on her own.

Clay, although taken in by the Colliers, still felt he had nearly always been on his own.

Because of each of their unique situations, they both felt years older than their true ages. Perhaps he was more advanced than Holly for he seemed ready to settle down. She — he wasn't so sure she was ready to make a home for a husband and all that came with it.

He respected her and warned his brain to calm the heat that was increasing in his groin.

One thing for sure, the two of them were in love. They both knew that. But she also knew if her father learned of their love, he'd have none of it.

A coal popped in the fire and she jumped, unlocking her

lips from his.

"Why are you so afraid to let your Pa know, Holly? Why do we have to hide to see each other?"

"Holly," a small voice wailed from the loft in the rafters of the cabin.

"Shh," she held her finger to his lips and studied Clay's face to make sure he realized the seriousness of one of the children waking up and finding him there. "Don't wake Bradley or Amy up, please. If we are very quiet maybe she'll go right back to sleep. I'll have a dickens of a time getting her back in bed if she gets fully awake."

"My Pa says you're a reckless maverick, Clay Bingham," she whispered and another soft giggle escaped her lips as though she liked the thought that he was a little rough around the edges. "If one of the kids sees you here, and tells Pa, he'll give me what for and come after you."

She gently pushed him toward the door.

"Now go, before we get into a mess with Pa." She reluctantly lifted the bar from across the door where she had rested it after he entered.

Clay was even more hesitant. He liked the feeling he got when she was close to him. He felt his manhood wanting to be satisfied and had to consider, when his brain was fogged with its demands, not to touch certain spots on her body he had in mind to caress.

"I love you Holly O'Flannery," he said as he squeezed through the small opening the door made as she held it ajar for him to leave. "Mark my words, one day you'll be Holly Bingham." He winked at her.

"Wait!" she stopped him. She hurried to the mantle where she had left a small gift for him. She handed him a tiny piece of needlework with his initials "CB," stitched into the material.

She had spent hours creating it and hoped he would be

25

pleased with her work.

He looked at it with curiosity.

"It's a good luck charm. Keep it in your pocket."

"I'll think of you every time I take it out," Clay promised. He was gone in a flash into the dark beyond the cabin.

~*~

Having reached the center of the buildings which were now made of sturdy materials instead of makeshift cabins and tents, he remembered the charm was long gone. It was missing from his pocket somewhere along life's path. Still, he didn't need it to bring to mind its creator.

The memories tore at him as he searched for a place for Buckshot to stand, temporarily.

He sheltered the bay beneath a building's lean-to while he sought a better place for the both of them.

That Christmas Eve seemed like an eternity ago and he hadn't seen Holly since their last encounter a few days after that. Not a day went by that he didn't think about her. He wondered constantly what happened to her. *What had she done when he was no longer around?*

She probably hated him for disappearing on her without so much as a goodbye kiss.

How could she know that he had wanted to swoop her up and carry her away with him?

How could she know that someone had killed his mentor, Captain Collier, and he was being blamed?

He was sure she must have found out later, after he left. *Heck, she may even believe he did it by now. Certainly her Pa would.*

Clay moved toward The Golden Saddle Saloon. Not because he needed a drink, but because he hadn't eaten all day since a chunk of beef jerky for breakfast. His stomach grumbled beneath his coat. Once he was at the door protected from the weather under the porch roof, he

26

removed his hat. He shook the snow from it and brushed the brim against his coat to remove what flakes had accumulated on his shoulders as well. He entered the saloon with apprehension heavy in his gut.

CHAPTER THREE

The warmth felt good when he stepped into the room where a small potbellied stove generated heat from its center. Around the edge of the interior, tables sat with their chairs turned upside down on top of them. A man wearing a filthy white apron swept dirt from a rough-hewn wood floor into a dust pan while two other men stood at the bar drinking. He dumped the sweepings of sawdust and grit into an open oak barrel alongside the bar out of range of tobacco-spitting cowboys and miners.

He moved back behind the bar and turned to Clay.

"Howdy, Stranger," he said.

"Howdy," Clay answered back glad to be considered an unfamiliar face. "Where is everybody?" He asked as his eyes looked over at the two men at the end of the bar. He hoped to reassure himself neither was Ian O'Flannery.

"It's pretty late, Mister. Most civilized folks are already home in bed, I recon'."

Satisfied that he was unknown by the men, Clay moved closer to the bar. He studied a sparse menu scrawled in white chalk on a large slate board attached to the wall.

28

The bartender sat the dust pan and broom aside and approached the bar to offer his services.

"Drink, Stranger?"

"Just coffee if you still got any."

"It's been sitting awhile. It might be camp brew by now — pretty strong and bitter, I suspect."

"As long as it's hot, that's all I care." Clay removed his worn leather gloves and cupped his hands together. He blew his breath into his palms to help dry his fingers where the snow had soaked through the seams of his cowhide gloves and turned his skin red. His hide was on the verge of changing to purple and he rubbed his hands together to revive the circulation. *Just holding the hot cup might help save his fingers from frostbite*, he considered as he waited to be served.

"You new to the area?" The bartender asked, then blew the dust from the bottom of a heavy mug. He wiped a cloth around inside and, finally, poured the thick black liquid to the cup's brim.

Clay studied the man. He'd seen him before when he lived at the Collier Ranch not far from there. He used to see him sweeping the front steps of the saloon sometimes when he came to town in the buckboard for supplies. Obviously, the man didn't recognize him. No surprise, as he hadn't frequented the town's social hubs. He'd done his business at the mercantile or blacksmith's shop and got back to the ranch as quickly as possible. Unless, he stopped to spend some time with Holly.

"Not so much. Been here before," Clay said not elaborating on his knowledge of the area.

"I'll take some of that food you got heating back there." Clay nodded his head toward the stove top where a mixture of coarse meat, onions and potatoes bubbled in a thick dark liquid in a cast iron pot.

29

He breathed in the aroma of the onions in the air mixed with the other scents and his stomach growled with anticipation.

"Didn't see stew on your board, but it smells good."

"Well, when most folks are through ordering for the day and there isn't much left, I toss what there is together and call it stew. It's passable if you're hungry enough."

"That I am!"

When the bartender sat the plate in front of him, Clay reached inside his coat and took a coin from his shirt pocket. He toyed thoughtfully with the currency, turning it in his fingers as he calculated his finances before paying for his meal.

"You know anything about an Ian O'Flannery?" Clay asked quietly so as not to be overheard by the other patrons. "I believe he used to live around here."

"Shoot. Most people know O'Flannery — Mr. O'Flannery," the man corrected himself in a stronger tone as if to indicate the man was an upstanding citizen or held a high position in the growing community. "Yep. He still lives here, only not where he did."

Clay looked up with surprise at the excited tone in the man's voice. His fork stopped in midair from where it was about to stab a chunk of potato on his plate. The slab of stale bread in his other hand paused part way to his mouth. The man he remembered didn't call for that kind of respect. *What had changed?*

"Hell, he went off up Virginia City way and hit it big there near Gold Hill. Built his self a big mansion at the end of the road with part of the money he's got. He hired some woman to look after his youngin's while he sent that oldest girl of his off to a finishing school back East. Whitman School for Girls, I believe it is. Highfalutin if you ask me. Even the name sounds like something that's got its collars starched too stiff."

Clay studied the man with curiosity. He couldn't believe what he heard.

The man stood behind the bar and rested has back against a counter made of a board across two metal bound oak whiskey casks. His blasting report about the O'Flannerys appeared to have exhausted him. He placed the palms of his hands on either side of his head and slicked his heavily pomaded dark hair back. Then, changing his mood again, he gloated as if having just scooped the local newspaper.

He relaxed his body and picked up the bar rag. Wiping his hands on it, he also wiped the top of the counter next to Clay's plate. He waited for Clay to comment.

Clay chewed his food while the news sank in.

"Heck, there's even been talk of calling this place a town and naming it Flannery," the bartender added as he gazed off as though reading his own future when even more settlers arrived to patronize his saloon. He especially favored miners who paid in gold dust, often over-compensating the man by their inebriated manner or generosity. He kept his hair heavy with the tacky pomade to catch each speck of gold dust that loosened itself from the miner's pouch. At the end of the day, he washed his hair to capture what flakes remained.

Clay ate his food slowly as he considered this burst of news recently fed into his brain. *So, Holly WAS gone. Well, he hadn't expected to run into her easily anyway.* As much as his heart tugged in the direction of the little cabin, he knew life wouldn't be the same as it was that Christmas Eve some time ago.

"Thanks, Mister," Clay said as he finished his food and drained the last bit of coffee from the cup. His body was thawed out now and his fingers and toes burned where the cold had been the worse. The pain matched the ache he felt in his heart at having lost Holly in the first place.

Well, good for ol' man O'Flannery, Clay thought as he looked for the best in the situation.

The family had suffered enough living from hand to mouth all those years. *And Holly?*

Well, that would sure make a big difference for her, not having to worry about the younger kids and getting the opportunity to become a fine lady.

A lady. She surely had passed him, a rough-edged cowboy and suspected killer, by. Even though they had thought themselves in love, now she'd probably not want to give him the time of day.

He envisioned Holly O'Flannery in a fine dress back East surrounded by slick, young men who had never earned calluses on their palms or worked a day's labor in their lives.

Clay bundled his coat and serape tighter around his body. He tugged his wet gloves back on for what little protection they might provide against the weather outside. He braced himself to return to the cold.

With Buckshot's reins in his numbing fingers he led the horse instead of mounting into the saddle. Slowly, he walked down the road toward the area he remembered where the cabin sat that housed the O'Flannery family before good fortune overtook them.

He wandered past the dark and dilapidated shanty and walked Buckshot a ways toward the end of town where the barkeep had said "Mr. O'Flannery" had built his fancy home.

Finally, Clay put his foot in the stirrup and raised himself into the saddle. Steam rose from Buckshot's body forming around Clay's legs and gear.

The snow had stopped falling. He looked up at the bright stars overhead where the clouds parted opening the sky up for view. The brightest star seemed right over the area where the O'Flannery house sat and he thought of the

Bible story of Jesus' birth.

It was the night before Christmas Eve.

The Christmas Star, he thought. *If only miracles still happened.*

Buckshot approached the two-story building surrounded by wrought-iron fencing.

Two carriage lights, one at each side of the gate, glowed atop each brick column that marked the entry. The gate, itself, was made of vertical square metal bars spaced a few inches apart. They were cut at different lengths to reach from straight bottom rails to scalloped top rails. A semicircle of metal was attached to the edge of each gate where it parted. Closed, now, they formed an "O." There was no doubt in Clay's mind this was O'Flannery's mansion.

Inside the house, soft light glowed through the fabric draped across the large windows.

So, this was Holly's new family home. Clay reined Buckshot at the gate and sat for a few seconds recalling happy times when he and Holly were together. He wondered if she ever came back from school to visit the family. He wondered if she ever thought of him.

A shadow of a woman's form moved across the curtains as someone walked between the lamp and the window of the house.

He doubted the figure was Holly. She was supposed to be at school. *It was a servant, probably,* Clay thought. Possibly the woman in charge of the remaining O'Flannery children.

Clay urged Buckshot on slowly, aiming for a boarding house he knew once stood near the livery stable. He hoped it would still be there after his lengthy absence.

It was late but the place had been cheap and he'd be out of the weather for the night, he reasoned.

Tomorrow he could start his search for answers to who

killed the Captain — and why they had blamed him.

If it wasn't him, as someone had charged, and he knew it wasn't, he'd be the only one to clear his own name.

What do I have to lose? I've already lost everything.

My parents.

My home.

My friend who treated me like a son.

And, my beloved.

Alas, what was he to do about any of it? For now, he felt he could do nothing but look for shelter out of the storm and away from prying eyes.

Ahead, Clay could see the outline of the boarding house, which also served as a short-stay hotel, in the dim light. Lanterns on either side of the doorway accentuated the entrance with its deer's antlers over the door and fanned a glow across the boardwalk in both directions.

As he moved toward welcome shelter, he felt sharp shafts of wind blow icy air through the threadbare spots in his clothing. He looked forward to getting inside out of the cold and wet weather. He wanted to dig some dry duds out of his saddlebags and get his slender body wiped down and warmed up before putting them on.

After a good night's sleep the morning should look better, he thought. He planned to meander down to the Barbershop, get a hair cut, have his beard, that had taken root for the last nine months, shaved off and soak in a tub of hot water before putting on his cleanest set of clothes. He hoped his dirty clothes would dry overnight before he had to put them on again to get to the Barbershop and his idea of luxury. He saw no point in wearing the fresher ones until after a bath.

"What can I do for you, Mister," a boy appearing only a few years younger than Clay greeted him as he turned the knob at what now bore a sign "Hotel Swanson."

After a quick glance inside, Clay pushed the door the rest of the way open.

"The sign says you have rooms to rent. I need one. Just for a night or two. Plan to move on as soon as I get warmed up from this storm and done relaxing in a tub to get cleaned up again. And, I need a stall for my horse in the livery," he added wanting to get Buckshot out of the weather as well.

"Sure. My Pa owns both the hotel and the stable. Think we can find a stall for the horse. You're just traveling through, then?"

"Don't intend to stay long." The inhabitants hadn't treated him well since the death of Captain Collier. He intended to spend no more time in this town than necessary.

Now that he knew Holly was gone, there didn't seem much point.

"Second floor. First room on the right upstairs," the young man said.

"Much obliged."

Clay paid for one night's lodging for both himself and Buckshot, not wanting to stay beyond that time unless he found a good reason to remain a second night. A good reason, he considered, would be any tip he could pick up that might help him figure out what happened to Captain Collier that made him a wanted man.

Before turning in, Clay followed the boy outside to move Buckshot to a stall where he would be warm, dry and fed. He removed his bedroll and lifted the saddle and blanket off the horse's back, setting them beside a pile of hay next to the stall. He gathered his saddle bags and slung them over his right shoulder.

"Anything else, Mister? If not, I need to get back in."

"No. You go ahead. I'll be right in. Don't worry about me, I can find my way back and upstairs to my room."

As he left the stable, he still could not shake the memories of his previous life.

He well remembered the night a mob of drunken men attacked him.

~*~

That night he had come to as if awakening from a nightmare, gasping from a sea of blackness, only to find out he had not been sleeping but living the horror. His head ached and his eyes refused to focus. Loud voices pulsed in and out in his brain — some so shrill the noise made his ears ache and his head hurt more.

Rough hands grasped his arms and dragged him toward a building. Now and then he felt a kick in his leg or his backside.

"What the Hell? I didn't do it! I just found him lying by the side of the road," Clay protested as he realized the previous activities of the evening. He defended himself for bringing the Captain's body in. He thought it strange, now, that a man had conveniently come upon him kneeling beside the Captain to see if he was still breathing. But, the man hadn't shown himself until Clay lifted the Captain onto Adonis's back behind the saddle. When he did, he forced him at gunpoint to ride into town ahead of him. It was a man Clay didn't recognize in the dark and assumed he didn't know.

When they reached town the man quickly set Clay up as the Captain's killer.

Although he protested, the local men grasped him tight and would have none of it.

"You's the last one to see Captain Collier alive. The fella that brought you in said you were there when he came upon you leaning over his dead body. Shut up and let the Sheriff sort this out."

That much was true. Captain Collier had ridden to town

on business that day. When night fell on the second day and he hadn't returned, Clay rode out from the ranch in search of the Captain.

He found him midway between the settlement and the Collier Ranch near the Carson River. Captain Collier lay on the trail dead. His great white horse was gone, along with the saddle bags that would have carried the cash the Captain went to town to withdraw from the bank had he been returning. The money was intended to purchase a new strain of cattle that would withstand the cold Nevada winters better than the breed ranging his land at the time.

Clay knew he planned to get enough money to pay for the herd along with a breeding bull of the same type. He knew it was a lot of money. But, he didn't know who else might be wise to the Captains plans. He certainly hadn't spilled the beans to anyone.

He had offered to go along, but the Captain insisted on going on the ride alone.

"I don't want to be responsible for anyone else's safety," he'd told Clay when he offered to be his protection. "I'll be fine. Nobody should know I'm carrying anything besides mail from the post office. I'll make sure I pick that up first. I already stuffed some old clothes in the bags so's they'd look full from the get go. I need you to stay here and protect Maggie."

Clay heard a rustle outside the bunkhouse. He raised a finger to his lips to warn Captain Collier they might be overheard.

"What?" the Captain asked in a whisper.

"I thought I heard something." Clay stepped to the door and moved to look around the side of the building. Whoever might have been out back was out of sight now. One of the ranch dogs ambled slowly toward him.

"What's up Buck?" Clay asked the dog as way of

acknowledgement and curiosity.

Buck stopped and scratched the back of his ear with his hind paw. *If there was someone around, they must be familiar to the dog,* he thought.

Clay walked back to where the Captain stood.

"Sure hope that was only Buck out there. I'd hate to think someone was spying on us. It wouldn't be good if anyone else knew your plans."

"You worry too much, Clay. You're as bad as Maggie. The wife's always thinking I put myself in too much danger. Hell, I told her, I always come back, don't I?"

Still, Clay worried. *Had someone been listening to their private conversation? It might have been one of the other wranglers. If it was, was he up to no good? Surely all of the Captain's men were trustworthy. Or, were they?* Clay wondered. *And, why didn't Buck raise a fuss if it wasn't someone he was used to seeing around the ranch? Must have been my mind playing tricks on me,* he decided.

Reluctantly, Clay agreed to stay behind even with concern still twisting in his gut.

When the Captain hadn't returned by late afternoon the next day Maggie Collier called Clay from the bunkhouse.

Her voice interrupted his work as he tried to finish up with the small herd of calves in the pen. He planned to recheck them to see if any were needing further attention.

"I'm afraid the Captain's plan may have failed, Clay. I told him he shouldn't go alone, but he wouldn't listen to me as usual."

"Nor to me, either. He wanted me to work that corral of calves instead of waiting until tomorrow," Clay said. "I'll ride out and meet him. He's sure to be close to home by now."

"Thank you, Clay. But, please, be careful, too. I'm afraid he might have come up on some road agent. They hit the train headed for Wadsworth last week. Got everything the people in the passenger car had on them. I do wish the Captain wasn't such a stubborn man."

"His stubbornness is probably what's got him this far, Ma'am," Clay said to reassure her as she shook her head and returned back inside the house.

Clay thought again about the subtle noise he had heard behind the bunkhouse earlier the day before. The batten boards barely screened any noise out of the sleeping quarters. He wondered if the dog could have been the culprit — *or was someone listening? Did someone overhear and take advantage of the information that the Captain would be carrying not only mail but a lot of money in his saddlebags on his way back from town?*

Now, he wondered at Mrs. Collier's words.

Had she had a premonition of the Captain's fate? Some people seemed to believe there were women who could see the future. Not that he bought into that bunk. But, worry seemed to have fretted her all day and, now, was Mrs. Collier sensing trouble, too?

In the days that passed since the Captain's death, he also wondered if Mrs. Collier had believed the gossip and rumors spinning around the locals. Surely, she, of all people, would know he would never harm those that took him in as a kid.

He'd never even been in a fist fight with another wrangler, let alone killed anybody. Besides, he had spent the day repairing tack and preparing to see that the calves were healthy before they were turned out to pasture away from their mothers. Weaning time was difficult. Had he not completed his task, the calves' bawling their heads off would have meant nobody at the ranch would have gotten any sleep.

Surely, Mrs. Collier had to know he was doing his job when she came to him for assistance in finding her husband.

He hadn't left the ranch all day until she interrupted his work to send him after the Captain.

As the mob, then, had dragged him down the dark street, he tried to protest his innocence. They seemed to have a vigilante mind and no individual listened to him. Mostly inebriated puny miners, they struggled to drag him toward the Sheriff's Office while Captain Collier's body lay still draped across Adonis's back.

The horse walked unfettered behind the group of men as they dragged Clay along. The mob stopped once to gather their strength. Adonis stopped as well. Several men took the Captain off the horse and let his body slide to the ground. One man remained there while his companions continued on with Clay in hand.

At least they appear to be heading toward the Sheriff's Office instead of taking the matter into their own hands, Clay thought. He was in no mood to be hung by vigilantes.

Adonis nickered behind him and, choosing between Clay and the other men who had relieved him of his burden, continued to follow Clay as he was forced along by the crowd.

Drunken as the men were, they staggered and swayed as they attempted to negotiated the street.

Two blocks before the Sheriff's Office, Clay took advantage of the men's alcoholic condition as they hesitated to pass a bottle around and quench their thirst from the job at hand. Clay surprised them and broke away. He burst past the stumbling, stupefied drunks.

His feet now steady beneath him, he ran into a dark alley where the blurry-eyed men lost him in the darkness.

Clay doubted any of the men would even remember what happened when they sobered up in the morning. He was counting on that as he worked his way through the alley and onto the road behind. Pressing his fingers to his lips he whistled shrilly to Adonis, his companion for a good many years. Adonis knew the signal. Clay knew it would bring him to his side, if his reins were still loose.

Adonis still stood, yet untied and unattended, in the dirt road. He turned his ears, getting directions from the sound.

Clay waited until he heard Adonis's running hoof beats, then he whistled again.

Getting his final bearings, Adonis raced to Clay's aid. Once they were horse and rider again, the two of them took off on a run toward the outskirts of the settlement in the opposite direction of the Collier Ranch. Clay left without so much as an opportunity to tell anyone who might care he was gone. Not Holly. Not Mrs. Collier.

~*~

Knowing what he now knew, as he relived that horrible night, he figured he didn't have a chance of reconnecting with Holly O'Flannery even if he tried. Not only had he left town without an explanation, her father probably felt sending her away was the best thing he could do to make her forget him.

Clay hadn't been much in favor with the man in the first place.

Alone on the trail, with not one witness to come forward and speak of his innocence, the finger of guilt pointed at him.

He knew, now that these men had accused him of killing Captain Collier, he was a wanted man. He grimaced at the image of the Captain's body that remained as a residual in his mind.

He rode out to the east, headed for Montana. North of the Collier Ranch, Clay stopped and opened a gate that enclosed the property line.

He slid from Adonis's saddle. He stripped Adonis of all his trappings. He swatted the buckskin on the rump.

41

"Home, Adonis," he shouted. "Go on home!"

In the dark he heard the sound of Adonis's hooves picking up speed. The sound diminished as Adonis put distance between them, making his way back to the barn.

Clay closed the gate and slung the saddlebags over his shoulder. He slid the halter up his arm, wrapping the reins under his armpit and over the edge of his shoulder, tucking the coil beneath the leather of the saddlebags. He picked up his bed roll and tied it tight beneath the saddleback before positioning the blanket and hefting it all on his strong shoulders.

Slowly, he started walking the trail that would, eventually, lead to a road where the stage ran to Winnemucca for connections north and east.

~*~

Clay pushed the memories away and went inside the warm hotel. He followed the clerk's earlier directions to his room for the night.

CHAPTER FOUR

Opening the door, hallway lamps threw enough light across the room for him to see a bureau to the left and a bed against the wall on the right. The room was so narrow there was barely a path between the two pieces of furniture. He noted a kerosene lamp on the bureau top with wooden stick matches in a container next to it. Knowing his bearings and the location of the lamp, he closed the door and secured it.

Letting his eyes adjust to the darkened room, he moved down the narrow space and fumbled for the matches. He removed the chimney from the lamp and, striking the sulfur end of the wooden match with his thumb nail, lit the wick.

Relieved to be out of the bitter cold weather, Clay stripped his wet clothes away from his chilled damp body and crawled beneath the covers to warm until he stopped shivering.

Thoughts of Holly refused to leave his mind as he shook beneath the blankets waiting for his core body heat to radiate out and form a cocoon of warmth.

Coming back had been a bad idea, he now thought. Not

only was it dangerous if anyone that knew him saw him until he could prove his innocence, it only exacerbated his thoughts of Holly. He had thought he could handle simply seeing her from afar. He thought that might help salve the ache in his heart. But, now, even that possibility seemed as remote as the tiniest star in the cold winter sky.

Clay wrapped the blanket around his body and went to stare out the small window toward the large house with the iron fence enclosure.

As Clay watched and tried to warm himself enough for sleep to take hold of him in his second-story room, down the street at the O'Flannery home a carriage pulled up to the entrance.

The driver stopped the team of chestnut horses and waited for a second male, an agile young boy, to step down and run to unlatch the gate. He held the reins tight to keep the team still while he waited for the boy to pull the gates wide and the "O" to separate and provide enough open space for the carriage to pass through. He drove the carriage through the gate past the young man, leaving him to close the gate behind them. When the gate reconnected to its locked position and the second male ran forward to climb back up alongside the driver, he urged the team on down the driveway.

"Whoa," the driver's voice called as he reined the animals once more to a stop beneath the sheltering overhang of the house. Quickly the young agile male, moved to assist the lone passenger from the fancy conveyance.

Clay wondered if it might be Ian returning after a drinking binge. A young woman crossed the lighted area the short distance between the carriage and covered entry. She stepped quickly out of the cold through the side door into the building.

The driver moved the carriage on down the path while

the young man rushed ahead to open the doors to the oversized barn next to a stable.

Inside the warm house the young woman walked through the darkened rooms and up the stairs toward her bedroom.

Holly was home.

It had been a long time since she slept in her own bed and, although it saddened her that her father didn't greet her, she was not surprised when the passenger with the driver was not Ian but, instead, the stable boy. She had wired Honora of her plans for the holidays so she knew the carriage would be waiting at the station to pick her up. She could count on Honora.

Through the years Holly learned she couldn't count on her father. She was used to his negligence of her emotions and his thoughtlessness toward her. *One would think*, she told herself, *that one would finally give up hope of eliciting anything beyond monetary support from the man.* She was coming to believe that she should never expect the normal. In all the years she had been alive, she had known only disappointment when it came to consideration from her father. *She should hate him for all that he put her and the children through before he became wealthy.* She willed herself not to think about the years of never having enough to eat while Ian O'Flannery numbed himself at one local saloon after another regardless what community they were living in. There were always more saloons than there were churches, or anything else for that matter.

But, then, her heart softened. She had nothing to complain about now, she reminded herself. She was sure the family would never have to worry about food or comfort again. Even if her father was often missing when important things occurred in the family — like her homecoming.

Ah well, she consoled herself. *She was sure he would be*

home when she arose in the morning.

She hesitated at her small sister's room, went inside and kissed the top of her blonde curls. Amy slept in luxury, now, as opposed to the cramped loft in the living quarters they left behind. Their former home sat empty and uninhabitable two streets over from where the train depot was constructed to accommodate travelers for the railroad and its trains that now ran cross-country.

She had turned her face away from that direction when she left the depot to avoid seeing the painful reminder of her previous life.

Stopping at Bradley, her young brother's room, she reached to pick up clothes he had strewn across the floor from the door to his bed. The lamp still glowed where he had fallen asleep reading a new novel, *The Adventures of Tom Sawyer,* before blowing out the flame. He could never have done that in the old place. For one, they could not have afforded the cost of the book. Two, his education, or lack of it, would not have offered the possibility that he could read well enough to enjoy such a story.

Holly removed the book from where it laid, pages open, text down and hardcover out like a small rooftop across his chest. She tucked the covers closer beneath his chin. She ran her hand over his brownish-red hair. He stirred momentarily. She turned the flame low and cupped her hand behind the lamp's chimney to blow the light out.

Yes, she decided, her father could be forgiven his transgressions. The children and the house were well cared for by Honora. Holly had opportunities she could not, once, have even dreamed of.

In the meantime, Ian O'Flannery's drinking habits had not changed. Now, he had even more time and money to spend on his pursuits. What surprised Holly was that he had managed to survive these many years with the amount of alcohol he consumed.

In the old days, she wondered at the safety of his negotiating the street between wagons, teams of horses and riders on horseback as he made his way home after a night of carousing.

Aside from that, she felt the liquor he drank was often poisonous. *He couldn't endanger his life more if he teased a disturbed rattlesnake*, she believed and had told him so on one occasion.

These days, the same carriage that transported her from the train to the house was often driven to drop Ian off at his bidding. On any "trip" the location of his choice was sure to be one of the several nearby saloons.

She well remembered a few nights after Christmas Eve when she last felt Clay's touch and gentle kiss. That cold winter night so similar to this, Ian had staggered through the cabin door to find her and Clay encircled in each other's arms.

~*~

"Get the Hell outta here," Ian shouted at Clay as he wove his way through the main room to his bed beneath the loft where the children slept. There he slammed the door and dropped onto his cot causing Amy and Bradley to stir overhead.

"And don't ever come back!" His words were slurred and muffled by the thick slab wood of the door between him and the startled couple.

Holly ducked her head and felt tears trickle down her cheeks. She was humiliated that her father had found her in Clay's embrace. Even more, she was angry that he had talked to Clay in such a manner.

Knowing that Ian would probably not be able to get up from the bed until he gained consciousness once more in the morning, Clay soothed Holly before he left.

"Don't worry. He probably won't even remember me being here by tomorrow," Clay said.

Holly nodded agreement to the possibility in the dim light from the dying embers of the fireplace.

"I am so sorry Clay. And so embarrassed — "she broke off.

Clay added more wood to the flames, giving himself extra time to consider what had just happened and calm his own nerves.

He returned to put his arms around Holly once more. He kissed her forehead. Holly clung to his side.

"It'll be all right, Holly," Clay assured her.

"I don't know how. But, we'll have to figure something out. He's just going to have to accept that we intend to be together."

He opened the door and slipped outside.

Holly watched as he rode Adonis down the street and turned toward the dark trail back to the Collier Ranch.

She never saw him again.

~*~

That was the last they saw each other. In the comfort of her new home, even to this day, Holly wondered why.

Now, as Holly reached her own room and sat on the side of the bed to remove her clothes she relived that night, again, in her mind.

What ever happened to Clay Bingham? She wondered as she lit her round glass-globed rose-painted lamp. She put on her nightgown and sat down at her vanity table to brush her hair and finish preparing for bed. Padding barefoot in her night dress, she remembered the rumors buzzing around town a few days later after her father had so rudely ordered Clay to leave.

When her father sobered up enough to prospect, again, he left without a word to her. The next time he returned home he was in another rage, having been without his favorite drink for days. He was, also, openly full of contempt for Clay.

He emphasized his dislike to Holly, "I tried to tell you that Bingham was trouble. Now, the fellas out prospecting say he's killed his boss. They said they had him caught red-handed the other night, but he got away."

"I can't believe Clay would kill anyone, let alone Captain Collier," Holly said in a state of shock as she defended him. "Is Clay all right? Where is he now?"

"Well, he's gone and good riddance," Ian O'Flannery spouted as he headed out to quench his thirst with another night of drinking. He left Holly on her own to deal with the misery she felt of not knowing what happened to Clay.

Did her father have something to do with his leaving? She vowed she would never forgive him if he did.

~*~

In Holly's room in the new mansion, hers was the sole window that emitted light now.

The flame of Clay's lamp was the only other bright spot that spread a glow through the one boarding house window.

Like the fingertips of two distant lovers reaching out to one another, the two illuminations stretched toward each other but fell short of merging in the middle of the street. The dark night air and distance between the mansion and the hotel was too far for the weak, yellow glow from their lamps to connect.

With one puff from the lips of each individual in the isolation of their lonely rooms, both buildings went dark.

Staring into the darkness, separated by only a short physical distance, both wondered — *Would they ever see each other again?*

CHAPTER FIVE

The following morning the sun cast bright rays from the edge of the earth as it poked its rim of fire up over the mountains on the eastern horizon. The storm had passed during the night leaving behind inches of snow that's depth varied depending on the elevation of the ground.

Clay awoke to the sun struggling to shine through the dirty glass window pane of the "Hotel Swanson." The glare was muted further by a filmy curtain that provided no privacy or protection against drafts. He moved from the warm bed with the patchwork quilt wrapped tight around him to look out and assess the area. Snow clung to roof tops and covered patches of the street where the lack of early morning traffic failed to erase it into puddles.

He considered that few people were eager to leave their warm homes and venture out into the accumulation of snow that fell over night.

The cold air soon seeped through the quilt and chilled any exposed parts of his body. He dropped the light curtain from his fingers and climbed back on the bed. He snuggled tight inside the patchwork-patterned material.

Clay considered the possibilities of his being recognized by anyone while he lay re-warming in the covers. It was comfort unlike any he had experienced in his days on the trail from Montana. It was a trip he didn't want to make again. He hoped to clear his name and be considered respectable once more. He had no desire to live further north and considered anything south of Reno to have weather too extreme in the opposite temperature.

In the time since his exodus, he knew his features had matured. Being younger then, he had sported a straggly mustache he coaxed to grow and fill in to no avail. Now, hair grew in places he'd rather it didn't. He had let his whiskers become unruly as a disguise. A clean shave should change his look to show that his jaw line had filled out as had his muscles. Hard work on the ranch had built and sculpted his entire body.

He hoped Buckshot, branded with the Montana ranch mark where he had worked after he escaped the drunken mob, would draw notice away from him. He no longer considered Adonis, who bore the Collier Ranch brand, his. He thought about the horse and wondered what had become of him.

Attachments, for Clay, were not easily dissolved.

To avoid the pain of the past, he let his mind go on to other things he could do to remain unnoticed. He'd keep his hat low once he'd finished his transformation at the Barbershop and hope he didn't run into anyone in public that might know him.

Having made his decision, he arose, again, from the warm covers. A chill shook his body as he reached for yesterday's dirty clothes. He pulled on his pants and shrugged into his shirt, both of which were soiled but dried stiff now, before padding barefoot to the window again.

He hurried back to where his saddlebags hung on the

metal edge of the bed frame. He reached into one saddlebag and pulled out a second pair of socks to cover the first and help keep his feet warm when he trudged through the snow and water outside the building to check on his horse.

He was unarmed, by design, so he had no hardware to take up space or add weight to his saddlebags. He was not out to look for a fight and, if he had to protect himself, he'd have to figure out a way to do it without a gun. Finding the Captain shot to death soured him on toting iron on his side.

Once fully dressed, he crossed the floor and gazed across the street and down toward the O'Flannery mansion again.

At the house, a white ribbon of snow clung to the top of the masonry columns like frosting running around the edge of a cake. Heat from the lamps during the night warmed the center of each of the columns to melt the snow and drip icicles from their caps.

He studied the house, which sat protected behind the ornate fencing, and considered whether the people inside would welcome a visit, should he decide to make one. He knew Ian O'Flannery might well take a shotgun after him. Perhaps he would run him off or kill him — if he were home. But, chances were he would be hung over and either sleeping late or already back at one of the saloons.

Unless he had changed his ways.

Clay considered that possibility while he watched a man snuff the lamps atop the columns out for the day.

Two children, probably Holly's brother and sister, ran to play in the snow behind the gate. He saw the door open and a woman come out to gather the children, he supposed, for breakfast.

Even from this distance he could tell it wasn't Holly. The woman appeared older and of a plumper, even shorter, stature.

With the activity gone, Clay turned away and thought of food for himself. He'd return to get his fresh duds once he saw that Buckshot had oats and hay for the day, too, he decided.

~*~

Holly, tired from her trip in from school, lazed in bed listening to the children's cheerful shouts outside the window and heard Honora call to them. There were several years between her and her younger siblings ages. Enough that she had always felt more like a mother to them than a sister.

Her own mother, being the wife of a miner, worked hard but held tight to her dreams of a better life for her children.

She chose their names for them from books she read or beauty she saw. There was a long list to pick from whenever a new babe was born.

Amy, the youngest girl, had been named after a painting she saw of a beautiful Christmas flower — an amaryllis. One of the wealthier parishioners of their church treasured the image and brought it to service to display during the holidays. Although the name was complicated to say, she found a way around that problem by writing the full name in their family Bible. Yet, for everyday purposes, the family simply called the little girl Amy.

Holly forbade her mind to wander where it did when she thought briefly of her mother.

Or, now that she was gone, to her memory. But, the mind, like the heart, takes directions from no one. Both follow their own paths. Holly thought about the tassel-topped redheaded woman that was her mother. She had been so young when she died. Both of them, mother and daughter, were so much alike in looks and mannerisms.

Being the eldest child of three live children, it was not

unusual for Holly to cling to her mother. She willingly helped her with the younger children and, eventually, tried to nurse her mother through a final miscarriage.

Holly watched her mother bravely fight to stay alive. She lay so quiet in her bed. Each day she grew paler.

On the third day, the tiny incompletely formed baby lay swaddled in a soft cloth within a discarded wooden cheese box, waiting to be buried when Holly's mother regained her strength.

Grasping Holly's hand her mother pleaded, "Take care of the others."

"Momma!" Holly cried realizing that all the doctor's efforts might be in vain. "No! Please...please don't leave me!"

The imperfect fetus was joined in death by their common parent. So that it would not be buried alone, it was placed in their mother's arms to rest in one grave.

There was no way for Holly to leave the younger children and find her father where he worked a claim in the mountains above their cabin. There was no way to get word to him, unless a miner that knew which claim he worked would deliver the sad news. For, according to some, he trekked to Virginia City where silver was more plentiful than gold.

One of the few stretches of time that Ian O'Flannery stayed out of town — stayed away from the saloons — he was oblivious to the tragedy playing out in his home where the family lived some distance away.

With help from some of the locals, Holly saw to her mother's burial along with the last of the O'Flannery offspring. She buried the pain of her loss and truly took on the role of mother to the smaller children.

She felt pain so severe she determined that, to survive, she must feel nothing. Never again would she feel love, anger or sadness, she vowed.

~*~

Now, she trembled beneath the warm covers as she tried to banish the ugly memories from her mind.

She no longer needed to worry about getting up and fixing breakfast for the children and seeing to their dressing for the day. The housekeeper, Honora, maintained not only the home but watched after the younger ones with competence.

Holly compared her new room to the old living quarters of three years ago. It, alone, was as large as the entire cabin they had all shared. Although she was uneasy with her family's new found wealth, she was happy that Amy and Bradley wouldn't have to grow up wanting as she had.

She knew the children still had rough edges from their former life living from hand to mouth with sometimes not enough to eat. She felt they were coming along well, growing healthy and educated, under the tutorage of Honora.

Born in Mexico, Honora had been sent away by her family to learn English prior to a raid on her home by bandits. She, away finishing her education, escaped their terror. Once she learned of her family's demise, she was advised not to return to her home but to escape to the north lest she, too, meet the same fate.

Eventually, her travels brought her to the small, but growing, settlement near where the Truckee River dumped into Pyramid Lake to the north and the Carson River bounded the land to the southeast.

Times were hard. But she heard rumor of one man who had struck it rich and was eager to hire someone to look after his children.

Ian O'Flannery, with his new found wealth, hired Honora to run his household and mind his children. It gave

him the freedom to live his own life without the tiniest
amount of guilt about ignoring his remaining family

Holly was grateful for her father's good fortune, but
apprehensive of the way people looked at her when she met
them in the store or on the walkways. Their expressions
were generally those of a cross between envy and shock.

It made her feel guilty for her fortuity. She felt she stuck
out when she was home in Nevada. When she was in
Boston, dressed in common with the other students, she
blended in. She was becoming more comfortable there. Yet,
homesickness refused to release its grip on her.

Holly smelled maple syrup as it warmed for the
pancakes and, for the first time in some days, noted hunger
in her stomach and a desire to eat.

It wasn't always easy to convince herself to go for food
at school. The overload of book work it took for her to stay
abreast of the other students caused her to miss out on
many things.

Not wanting to fall behind, she struggled to catch up
from the start after having a poor opportunity as a child to
keep up with chores as well as school. There simply was
little time for an education then. By the time she could
attend the one-room schoolhouse, her mother's health was
failing and she needed Holly home to help with the children.

Then, losing her mother early when the children were
but babies, Holly soon left learning behind all together and
mothered the younger ones. Now, handicapped by her poor
education, she struggled to maintain equality in her studies
with the other students.

She knew this was her chance to become an educated
woman. She aimed to be one of Nevada's first women
lawyers. With the responsibility of Amy and Bradley off her
shoulders, she now dared to dream. And not just ordinary
dreams, but magnificent ones as well.

There was a light tap on her door.

"Miss Holly," Honora called.

"Yes?"

"Breakfast is ready."

"Will Papa be joining us?"

"May I come in?" Honora asked.

"Of course."

Honora pushed the door open gently.

"Miss Holly, your Papa has traveled away. Across the ocean. To England, he said. Maybe Ireland or France."

"Oh," Holly answered in surprise but without much emotion. "I'll hurry and dress so the children won't have to eat alone."

"Thank you, Miss Holly. They miss you when you are away. It would be good if you could be here for a time while your father is gone." Honora turned and left to tend to the food in the kitchen.

Holly rose from her bed and quickly freshened up and dressed for breakfast.

It felt good to her to pull a warm flowing calico dress over her body. She had trouble getting used to being cramped into the stiff school uniform of a starched white blouse and a long black skirt required for classes.

When the holidays approached, she had chosen to take the long train trip home, even if it would mean only a few days there before returning to school. She missed the slower pace of Nevada.

Here, with bigger goals in mind than an uneasy marriage, she wasn't driven by the other women's competition for the gentlemen that came to call after classes in the East. Her main passion was the siren of the legal field.

Although, as a woman, she was unable to vote or hold deed to her own property in her name if she married, she adamantly believed that the position of women attorneys, rare as they were, would, one day, provide an opportunity for her to join their ranks. Taking a stance in a male-dominated profession was a first step to seeing that, someday, she would have equal rights with men.

At first, when her mother died, Holly thought she would never allow herself to be hurt again. But she found out years later, refusing love when it approached out of nowhere was impossible for her to do.

Holly was a loving person. As such, she was also vulnerable.

When Clay left without warning, she decided life was more valuable to her to be someone with a career than to marry some other man she didn't love and bear his children. So, when her father struck it rich, she gladly went away to school rather than deal with the suitors that came calling. Her mind hungered for the education of which her previous life had starved her.

Her father, more interested in introducing her to the dandies back East than having her married to a rough and tumble cowboy, saw to it that her financial needs were met.

As far as he was concerned, as long as she stayed in school and didn't bother him about his life style, or become interested in some poor Nevadan that might expect him to share his fortune, she could study anything she wanted.

Good luck to her ever getting anywhere with her big ideas about becoming a lawyer, Ian O'Flannery thought. He supposed, *next, she'd want to be a judge or join the legislature or who knew what!*

Before packing and taking the stage to San Francisco where he boarded a ship for Europe, Ian O'Flannery had arranged for his younger children's Christmas presents to be built and delivered to the estate in time for Christmas morning.

As in years past, again it would be only Holly and his other two children for Christmas this year. His presence would be replaced with special gifts he was sure the children would like and, while they cushioned the hurt of his absence, he would feel less guilty for ignoring his family during the holiday. *What did they need him there for, anyway? He was now able to provide for them without the struggles of the past. Shouldn't that be enough?* He rationalized his departure.

With her father gone, Holly was even more determined to stay home during the full holiday break then before. She feared the youngsters might feel totally abandoned during the season if neither of their elder relatives joined in the celebration. She had always been the one to share their delights on Christmas morning since her mother died. *She was the one to see their joy at the treats and toys Clay had brought that last Christmas Eve* when he was still in town.

Ian traditionally joined the unattached men at the saloon for his day even when he was nearby, family or not.

That is my lot in life, Holly thought and put her disappointments aside. She decided, when her father ordered, more than suggested, she go to school, with the opportunities money allowed she would improve her life and build a career that did not depend on her father's approval of her choices. She was determined someday to be free to make her own decisions.

She finished braiding the sides of her hair and pinned two pigtails to the center at the back of her head over the remaining hanging tresses. With one last glance in the mirror, she left to join the family downstairs.

"Holly," the children shrieked when she entered the kitchen. Not knowing that she had arrived late the night before while they slept, they were surprised to see her sit down at the table and join them for breakfast.

"Did you see the Christmas tree?" Amy asked excitedly from her place at the table. "Do you think there'll be presents there Christmas morning?"

"Yes. And, yes." Holly reached to squeeze the precocious five-year-old's chin.

"You are growing so big!" She said to Amy. "And, you, Bradley, you are quickly becoming a young man."

The eight-year-old boy ducked his head.

"I'm hoping for a sled that I can take to the hill and ride while the snow lasts," he said to distract his sister from focusing on his growth progress.

"And, I want one that looks like a swan," Amy stated. "Have you seen one like that, Holly? Papa says there is no such thing. That it would be a miracle if ever anyone saw one. But, that's what I want. That's all that I want. I want to be able to slide down the hill near Spangle's pond in a swan. Do you think I will?"

Amy was tiny for her age, hardly weighing more than a small sack of sugar. *And just as sweet,* Holly thought. There was no doubt in her mind, if Amy had a swan sled she would glide effortlessly down the hill. Holly encouraged the child's whimsical mind.

"You just keep on dreaming. I'm sure there must be one out there somewhere!"

But, would she ever see her own dreams realized? She wondered with apprehension heavy in her heart.

CHAPTER SIX

"Good morning," the woman that ran the boarding house spoke as Clay came down the stairs into a foyer where warmth seeped into the room from the adjoining kitchen. Heat from the cook stove helped take the chill from the morning air.

"Good morning," Clay answered respectfully.

"Would you like breakfast before you go out?"

"Yes. Please," Clay maintained his manners.

"There's scrambled eggs, bacon and coffee on the sideboard in the dining room where our steady boarders eat. Help yourself." The woman left quickly as if on her way to take care of some important errand.

Clay walked into the dining room. There he nodded to the two other men the woman had referred to as boarders. They sat at a large round oak table partially covered by a small square tablecloth that was turned askew. The edges of each corner draped over the table rim letting the luster of the polished bare wood shine through its triangular gaps.

The men sat opposite each other. They nodded back in acknowledgement as they chewed their food. Their mouths appeared to Clay to be too full to speak. Surely, that was an indication how tasty the meal might be.

Regardless, it would be a treat to have eggs for a change. Since most people's chickens stopped laying with shorter daylight, that the cook even managed to serve eggs surprised him. But, he guessed he'd know if they had been in storage until they went bad when he tasted them.

Clay took a cup from a stack on the sideboard and poured strong, hot coffee into it. He sat it on the table, claiming his place, as he moved back to get a plate and fill it. Hunger gnawed in his stomach and he eagerly set the plate, laden with food, down and positioned himself onto a wooden chair at the table near the sideboard.

A fat man, dressed in a dark blue paisley vest and solid blue suit, occupied the chair at the end of the table. His girth was squeezed tight between the chair's curved wooden arms and his hips protruded out between them and the seat. He cleared his throat.

"I'm Tyler Washington. I own the bank here."

Clay nodded a silent greeting at his introduction.

The second man, dressed in a rawhide jacket so new it still put off a scent and stitched heavy with fringe cut from strips of the material, moved his feet from beneath the table to rise and refill his plate.

When he stood, Clay noticed he wore fancy silver lady-leg spurs attached to weathered boots. The rowels were quieted by pieces of cork he had wedged in each of them.

His hair hung down below his ears and a mustache sat above his upper lip. A scraggly beard jutted from his sharply tapered chin. The man appeared gaunt enough to make Clay wonder if the food he stuffed in his mouth did anything to put meat on his bones. The man looked like an image on a poster Clay had once seen. Whether he was related to the model for that or trying to emulate the man that posed for it, it was hard for Clay to figure.

With no introduction forthcoming from this strangely attired man, Clay ate his meal in silence and wondered about both of these two men.

The banker seemed sincere enough. But, why was he living in a boarding house if he owned the only bank in town? He must have enough money to build or buy a home of his own.

The other? Clay puzzled over him in his mind. Was he a dandy? A lawman in disguise?

He saw no badge showing. Perhaps the man was a bounty hunter? Clay felt distrust turn in his gut. If he hadn't run afoul of the law over what happened to Captain Collier, Clay realized he wouldn't be so suspicious.

Between bites, Clay continued to study his breakfast companions. Whoever they were, he wasn't convinced either one of them was who he claimed to be.

"Excuse me," the banker said. He struggled up from his chair, dislodged his overhang of fat from beneath its arms, and prepared to leave the dining table.

"Got to get to the bank and open it so folks can get to their money before we close for Christmas Day," he said as he lifted his hat from a peg on the wall and positioned it on his balding head.

The man in the rawhide jacket watched him go without responding.

Clay finished eating and cleared his plate to a small stack of dirty dishes nearby on a cart.

As he left the room he felt the stranger's eyes turn on him as if their boring into the back of his head would release information from his brain. He sensed a prickle in the hair at the nape of his neck.

"Hey! Mister," the man called after him.

Clay hesitated. Slowly he turned toward the man.

Was he calling him out?

Unarmed, he had no defense if he did threaten him. He hadn't seen a gun belt on the man. Like so many boarding houses the policy was to leave weapons locked in their safe until the guests left. Clay had paid no attention to any notice that might have been posted since he wasn't carrying firearms. *Even if there was a rule against having them inside, would this man obey the rules?* Clay doubted it.

Clay said nothing. He looked into eyes as dead as those of yesterday's trout.

"Don't I know you?" The man asked.

"I don't believe so."

"Something about you is familiar. Just can't say what. Yet."

Clay acknowledged his comment with a nod and turned to leave.

"When I come up with it, I'll let you know."

Clay glanced back as the man waved his fork in the air toward him. Without further hesitation, Clay made his way to the counter in the lobby.

I better get the heck out of here before he does figure out who I am. Clay took a deep breath and let the air release slowly through his nose. *The last thing I need, right now, is for someone to connect me to the situation I was in when I left town before.* He checked his stride for confidence as he moved away from the dining room.

He hesitated to check out before going to his room to pick up his things.

Then, something changed his mind. Why should he let words of a stranger form his plans? *This is crazy*, the voice in his head countered. *Just grab your stuff and get out! Don't risk trouble by sticking around!*

It was Christmas Eve. He could just as easily ride out on Christmas Day. He didn't know what held him there aside from a chance to clean up as he had planned. Or was it his memories of Holly and that holiday period a few short years back? *Something sure was telling him not to leave.*

"Can I help you, Sir," the young clerk asked.

"Yes. Sign me in for another night, will you?"

Stubborn, that's what some people might say I am. But, he wasn't ready to move on. Not yet.

He went quickly to his room to avoid the stranger still at the table where he left him.

Through the window in his upstairs room he saw Tyler Washington unlock the door of the bank and go inside. A shade rolled up behind the window where "Settlers' Bank" was painted in gold lettering on its glass.

Clay gathered his saddlebags with the fresh clothing and headed for the hot, soaking bath he planned to enjoy at the local Barbershop.

Descending the stairs he saw the man in rawhide exiting the small dining room. Clay stepped back behind the wall where the stairway took a right turn at a landing and waited until he heard the bell attached to the front door jingle. The door closed and Clay looked around the corner to make sure the stranger had left the building before moving downstairs to the lobby.

Not wanting to appear suspicious himself, Clay opened the door smoothly. He looked about cautiously before stepping onto the narrow boardwalk.

The man he was concerned about was nowhere in sight.

A small crowd gathered across the street at the bank.

Traffic moved up and down the muddy main street as horses' hooves and wagon wheels splashed snow into dirty slush while people went about their business.

Avoiding the congestion, Clay walked around the side of the boarding house and into the stable in back of the hotel. His purpose was two-fold. One, he didn't expect to run into the man in the fringed jacket taking this route. The other, he planned to make sure his horse was still there and being well cared for.

His earlier plan to check on Buckshot had been sidetracked by the woman's offer of a hot breakfast. Now, he felt a slight twinge of guilt for not looking after the animal's needs before taking care of his own.

He remembered Captain Collier had always told him, "Take care of your horse first. You take care of him and he'll take care of you."

He knew the Captain was right. Without the horse, he would be stranded. Afoot he wouldn't be able to escape if someone did connect him with his past.

Inside the livery stable the sweet smell of hay drifted in the air. Near the back, Clay could hear someone scooping a shovel against the floor. Occasionally the odor of manure mingled with that of the feed.

"Howdy, Mister," a young boy called out. "Which horse is yours?"

"Howdy, Button. The bay over there," Clay answered.

"I done mucked his stall out and fed him. He's a nice horse. I even gave him oats this morning, he was so quiet. If you're wanting to take him, he's ready to go."

"No. I'll leave him here for the time being. Here's a coin for you, though, if you'll take him out to the water trough for me and see that he's kept fed and watered 'til I am ready to leave."

"Thanks, Mister." The boy bounced the coin in his open palm contemplating the money.

"That's usually included in what you already paid up front in the hotel." He cocked his head and waited to see if the man would retract his offer. "My brother should have told you that when you checked in."

So the smaller boy got stuck with the stable chores, Clay

thought. *Wonder how his brother worked that one out?*

"Can't say that he mentioned it. Keep it, anyway. Then I'll be sure my horse has regular care." Clay waved his hand in the air. "It's yours. Say, have you seen a fellow around here wearing a new buckskin-colored jacket with fringe at the bottom and down the arm seam?" Clay asked with nonchalance.

"Yep."

"Do you know who he is?"

"Nope, but he had some fancy spurs. Lady-legs I heard another fellow call 'em, and a holster with two guns in it."

"Think he's an outlaw, Button?"

The boy studied Clay for a minute. A glint of joy came into his eyes. "If he is I sure hope I don't miss out on any excitement he causes while I'm stuck in here shoveling manure from the stalls."

"You hear anything, let me know will ya?"

The boy calculated how much he might have to do to feel he'd earned the coin the guest gave him.

He shrugged. "Guess so. But I don't know if I'll be wandering around much. Leastwise, not 'til I get my work done here. Ma don't let me out much. And my brother is sure to snitch on me if he finds out."

Clay nodded. "I'm not expectin' much. There might be another coin in it for you if the information is worthwhile." He hated asking the boy to poke around, but there was no other choice. If the man saw him again, he might remember where they'd met. The kid was less conspicuous than he was.

"Yes, sir!" The boy eagerly agreed.

Clay turned and walked back toward the stall door, stopping momentarily to rub the soft-skinned area of his horse's nose with his fist before he tugged the stable door open.

CHAPTER SEVEN

Clay left the stable behind and moved down the boardwalk toward the Barbershop with vigilant steps. He couldn't shake the feeling that the stranger in the rawhide jacket was an even bigger threat now that he knew he was armed. He didn't know why nor how he'd find out but, he decided, it might be a piece of information that could help solve the mystery of who killed Captain Collier. And, if it did, he hoped it would clear his own name once and for all.

He passed the Settlers' Bank on his way to get his shave and bath. He glanced through the window and saw Tyler Washington sitting in a small alcove with the office door open.

A teller waited on clients at a metal-barred opening above an enclosed counter. The cage served as protection for the teller if ever there was a dispute between him and clientele. Or, if the bank was robbed.

Next to the bank was the assay office followed by the saloon where Clay had first stopped the night before.

In front of the saloon another young boy, bundled up in a heavy coat that appeared to be fashioned out of saddle blankets, sat on the steps panning gold from the previous night's sawdust sweepings. Clay nodded to him when the boy looked up from skillfully working the pan to wash the sawdust into a float on top while the gold dust dropped to the bottom of the pan.

Clay remembered the bartender wiping his hands through his heavily-greased hair. *I bet that's the way the man collected spilled gold. He must pick up stray dust off the bar with the rag he wipes it with, too.* The boy laboring over the gold pan put the pieces together in his mind for him.

Oftentimes, when a miner paid with a pinch of gold dust some fell on the bar. More, if he was already drunk. Clay had seen it happen. The drunker the miner became, the more careless he was. It was to the proprietor's advantage to keep pouring the miners drinks.

Little did Clay know that, when the man wiped the bar, what dust fell to the floor was picked up by shoes he purposely muddied at the beginning of his shift. Later, he washed his hands and hair into a basin. This he followed with the mud from his soles containing what gold dust was stuck in the muck.

Between these methods and the floor sweeping, the bartender was able to make a nice chunk of money when he took the free gold to the Assay Office.

Clay had never had the experience of spending gold dust. He'd been a cowhand since he was young. He'd never been a miner, nor had a desire to be one. He liked the smell of horse flesh and the squeak of saddle leather when he rode across the range. The solitude gave him peace of mind and time to think. *Sometimes, too much time,* he thought now.

Lately, his mind had become too busy with memories of Holly.

Turning away from the boy busy at his task, he stepped

up and glanced over the swinging bar doors exposed to daylight, now, with their outer protective doors blocked to the side. He scanned the backs of the men standing at the bar while a different bartender facing him poured drinks for them. The second man from the left in the group was the man in the new-appearing rawhide jacket.

Clay quickly stepped to the side of the door and listened intently trying to detect anything that might give him a clue as to who the man was.

The boisterous voices of the men meshed together. Clay was unable to decipher who was talking or if it was the man that interested him.

The boy rose and went inside to deliver the gold dust to the owner, who had also been last night's bartender. Now, in his back-room office the boy received a pittance for his efforts.

The Barbershop and Bath House was at the end of the rutted street and Clay hurried toward it.

"Howdy," the Barber said as he pushed through the door. Looking for a shave and a haircut?" He sized Clay up for his needs.

"Yes. Then, line me up for a tub of hot water to soak in," Clay answered.

"You bet, Mister."

The man walked toward the rear of the building where a wide blanket partitioned off a small space for privacy.

"Wong Cho. Gentleman out here wants a bath. You got that water hot, yet?"

"Yes, Boss. I heat more."

While the Barber clipped at his hair, Clay heard quick footsteps shuffling behind the partition.

The sound of water sloshing from one vessel to another soon came to him as the hot water poured from a bucket into a larger container. As the bath tub filled, the sound changed its pitch.

At last, the water level reached its required depth.

Wong Cho called out, "Water ready, Boss."

Clay heard the back door close and the Barber put down his razor and removed the cloth he had placed around him when he sat down. He motioned for him to enter the area behind the flimsy cover. There the dim light showed steam rising from the copper tub as a small stove radiated heat into the bathing area.

Clay hung his saddlebags on a nail someone had driven into the wall and removed his clean clothes from them to hang on the next nail over. He removed his dirty clothes and rolled them, inside out, into a bundle before setting them on a dilapidated chair nearby.

Clay studied the drying cloth hanging by its corner on a third nail. It looked like a ragtag piece of an old quilt top that came across country in a settler's covered wagon. *Hell, it looks like it laid out in the Forty Mile Desert and got bleached in the sun, then, maybe, dragged behind the mule before being tossed aside.* Somehow the Barber got hold of it, must have washed it up and made use of it for cowboys to dry off after their soak. Ragged as it was, Clay was sure he would appreciate its use when the time came.

Carefully, Clay eased himself into the hot water. He felt the soothing liquid inch its way up his legs as he tempered his body to its heat until he, at last, eased his tall, trim form in up to his neck in the water.

Too tall for the length of the tub, Clay lay back, letting his knees poke out of the water, and savored a feeling of relaxation he hadn't enjoyed in a long time. The warmth lulled him into a doze and he let himself succumb to its invitation.

The sound of the front door of the Barbershop opening creaked into his relaxed sleepy haze. Clay heard the Barber greet the customer as he stirred.

"What can I do for you, Fella?" The Barber asked.

"Give my beard and mustache a trim." The voice replied.

"Sure thing. Take a seat right here."

Clay heard the Barber's cloth snap in the air as he popped loose hair from previous customers to the floor.

"You care to take off your fancy jacket first?"

"Naw. Just cover it up good," the voice replied.

Clay thought he recognized the voice and tensed a bit. *Was it the man from breakfast? Or was he still jumpy from his earlier encounter?* He waited for something that would confirm or deny it.

"Mighty nice looking rawhide you're wearin'," the Barber's words came to him.

"New. Fresh smell. Don't see many people wearin' somethin' like that around here." The Barber seemed to be making general conversation with the customer.

Did the man follow him after all? Clay wondered.

He heard the chair squeak as the Barber adjusted the customer to tilt him back and work on his facial hair.

"Trim the sideburns, too, while you're at it."

"Yes, sir. Will do. What brings you to our little place?" The Barber asked, having recognized him as a stranger to town.

"Just minding my own business," the man replied. It was an insinuation that told the Barber he should heed his words, too.

The chatter stopped.

The water in the tub cooled and Clay wanted to get out before it became too cold and chilled his body. But, he hesitated, not wanting to show himself to the customer as the Barber worked.

The Barber nodded his head but Clay couldn't see the

action. Like Clay, the Barber took the stranger's comment as one to tell him to mind his own business and shut up.

Clay wished the man had given some reason for being there that would have alleviated his concerns.

Slowly, Clay rose from the tub and removed the largest coarse bit of cloth from the nail above the decrepit chair. He wrapped it around his body at his waist. He stood close to the stove while he dried off with a matching piece of patchwork material that appeared to have been torn from the first.

The Barber finished shaving the man's sideburns.

"You want I should trim up your hair, too?"

"Nah," the man ran his hands along the sides of his head and down the back to his neck.

"Think I got a bit more time before I need to get that done."

Clay heard the cover cloth snap the air again and knew the Barber was finished.

"All done. You want to look in a mirror?"

Clay peeked through a crack between the fabric partition and the outside wall.

He saw the man take the hand mirror from the Barber. He turned to get the best lighting on the glass he could to see the results.

"Looks fine." He dug into his pocket and flipped a coin in the air for the Barber to catch.

Before handing the mirror back, he took another look. Turning so the reflection in the glass picked up the image of the partition, he stood studying the back of the room in the mirror's image.

Clay squeezed tighter to the wall and stood quietly.

"The sign says you got baths here, too. I gather that's behind the curtain over there," the man said as he lowered the mirror.

Clay held his breath as he heard the man's boots move closer.

"Yeah. You interested? There's a bit of a wait. The Chinaman has to heat more water."

"Not right now. Maybe later. I'll come back if I am. Here's your mirror."

Clay heard the footsteps recede and the door close after them.

Once he was sure the man was gone, he gathered his clothes and dressed quickly.

He looked around the hem of the curtain, again, before he walked into the area where the Barber's chair sat.

The man was busy sweeping up the stranger's clippings, with the rest of the morning's debris, into a pile on the floor.

"Thanks. The soak felt good," Clay told the Barber as he paid for his services. All the while he kept watch out the small window of the shop.

Be my luck the guy'd come back, he thought as he sought to catch a glimpse of the man or tell in anyway which direction he had gone.

For now, Clay moved outside and turned away from the main stores in town, knowing full well it would take him past the O'Flannery house.

Better that than have a run in with the stranger before he knew what he was up against, Clay rationalized. But his heart was pounding inside his chest as he thought of the possibility that he might glimpse some small bit of information about Holly even if it was only to know what a fine house she now had to live in with her new life.

He shifted his saddle bags over his right shoulder and kept his left arm free. He had no weapon beyond his fists and they were not of much benefit.

Clay joined a crowd walking down the roadway across the street from the O'Flannery mansion. They slowed their steps as they gawked at its magnificence as the biggest house in the area. It gave him time to study the building as well. He heard low conversation between two women about its occupants and wondered where Holly was this Christmas season.

Probably married already, reason told him.

There was no one to ask without compromising his safety. No way to find out, for all he could figure.

He moved across the street and walked toward the first store building.

A young woman in the family way moved toward him. He could see her large belly protruding between the gapping edges of her outgrown coat. The dark brown material of her dress pulled taut across the bulge as if to split open if the baby grew much more.

Maybe Holly had children. This girl was, perhaps, even younger than Holly. *It was best if he put thoughts of her behind him. A pretty girl like Holly didn't stay single long.*

Suddenly, gun shots rang out.

Clay clutched the young, pregnant woman and pushed her into the entryway of the first structure they came to. She looked at him with shock showing in her eyes.

"Sorry, Ma'am." Clay dropped his hands from her arms and moved between her and the edge of the building. "You best go on inside or see if you can take shelter in the alcove there."

As she moved away from him, he ducked down behind an upturned whiskey barrel and looked for the source of the gunfire. Knowing the girl was as safe as she could be, Clay studied the length of the road for the location of the shots.

"Sheriff," a voice called out. "The bank's been robbed!" A man raced down the street periodically taking protection behind pillars and alongside doorways. "Sheriff!"

The local Sheriff raced toward the sound of the gunfire.

The man pointed back at the bank building but only exposed his arm long enough to direct the Sheriff.

On foot, the Sheriff was bound to be outdistanced quickly by the robbers. He hesitated and untied the reins of a nearby horse in front of the saloon.

He mounted a strange horse, commandeering it for the chase, and raced toward the Settlers' Bank.

Silence fell in the street and Clay decided that the robbers must be gone.

The Sheriff dismounted in front of the bank.

Clay rushed toward the excitement, momentarily forgetting his vulnerability. At last, he hung back and watched from a short distance away.

A crowd milled around outside the bank building like so many cattle waiting for feed.

Tyler Washington paced back and forth on the boardwalk in front of his bank's doorway. His eyes were wild with fright and his rounded face was pale from the episode and his narrow escape.

"He shot at my teller, but missed," he explained to the Sheriff. "Got several hundred dollars at that. Maybe more."

"What'd he look like?" The Sheriff asked.

"I couldn't tell. I was in my office. All I saw was the back of his head. Of course he had his face covered. I could see the knot of the bandana in the back of his hair. Light colored hair — dirty blonde you might say. Thought it was strange he was wearing only a light shirt in this weather. He jumped the teller and rushed out the door before he knew what happened. William said he shoved what money was in the drawer to him and ducked when he raised his six-shooter. Got two bullet holes in the ceiling of the bank where he shot over William's head and into the wood anyhow."

"When I rushed out of my office all I saw was smoke and smelled gun powder. When I reached the door I saw the fella racing out of town to the south on the back of a dun-colored horse with a dark mane."

Tyler Washington went back inside the bank shaking his head. He turned the sign in the window to "Closed" and locked the door before the crowd dispersed.

"Now, folks," the Sheriff said once they were all outside in the brisk air, "don't worry none about your money. I'm sure, soon's Washington gets a tally, he'll open back up so you can get what you need. In the meantime, I'm forming a posse to go after the bank robber. Who's willing to ride with me?"

The Sheriff reached down on the boardwalk and picked up a scrap of rawhide material less than an inch long. He rolled it between his thumb and forefinger and studied the piece as the crowd dispersed.

Clay wanted to get closer to see if what the Sheriff held was what he thought it was. The Sheriff reached out and touched the spike of a nail that had been driven through the hitching rail at an angle that left the sharp end exposed and protruding from its post.

Clay ignored the Sheriff's request and pondered Washington's comments as well as the small fragment of light-colored rawhide the Sheriff had picked up.

He wondered if his breakfast partner could have been the one that robbed the bank. If he was, perhaps he had no more to worry about. *Surely, the man wouldn't come back. He'd get away as fast and as far as he could,* Clay reasoned.

He determined to watch for the unfriendly stranger. If he didn't see him again, he'd figure he was the bank robber and he wouldn't be around to bother him.

If Clay had followed the rider's tracks in the snow he would have found, not too far from the Barbershop, the stranger stopped. He dropped the horse's reins and dismounted. He pulled his fringed jacket from his saddle bag and unrolled it, donning it against the cold.

Swiftly, he removed the bridle and saddle from the horse and put them on a spare horse he had hidden earlier in a thicket for his convenience. He freed the first horse into a farmer's snow-covered pasture with other animals. He mounted the fresh horse, a flashy pinto, and rode back to the populated area. Nonchalantly, he tied the pinto up behind the Barbershop

While all the townspeople were abuzz about the robbery, the thief soaked in the copper tub in the back area of the Barbershop. He smoked a large cigar while he sat up to his armpits in hot water. Chuckling to himself, he blew smoke rings into the air above the front brim of his brown cowboy hat that was still on his head.

"Hey, Barber, get that Chinaman to bring me some more hot water." He flicked his ashes onto the sudsy-water-splashed floor. "This damn pool is getting cold."

He leaned back to relax while he waited for more soothing hot water to mix with the cooler water in the tub. Like something a man can't get enough of, the water although hot, was not hot enough and each time his body adjusted to the temperature he bellowed for more hot liquid.

Wong Cho scurried back and forth like a pantry rat dipping the cooled water from the tub with the bucket and reheating it to pour back in.

At last the man stopped calling for water and raised himself up in the tub. He stood for a minute enjoying the last of his cigar before wrapping himself with a scrap of cloth left at the side of the tub for him.

He shook one foot free of as much water as he could before stepping onto the floor. Once he had his balance, he raised the other foot and shook it. He did this, not because he was neat and wanted to spare the Chinaman more work, but because he didn't want to have any more water to wipe from his feet than necessary.

Damn scrap of cloth don't seem thick enough to dry my body, much less my legs and feet, he muttered to himself. *For the price of a soak, you'd think they'd supply a better rag to rub off with.* He complained under his breath and vowed to buy himself something that would serve better to dry on for the next time he enjoyed a good bath.

His rawhide jacket hung on the back of the rickety wooden chair while he dressed.

Once he pulled his shirt and pants on, he looked into a piece of broken mirror that hung by a wire on a nail hammered into a stud nearby. With both hands he slicked his hair back on the sides and assessed his reflection. The man slid his arms into the jacket.

He was confident, actually cocky, in his belief that no one recognized him at the bank or when he rode out of town.

He tugged his boots back on and adjusted his spurs. Having removed the corks from the rowels when he switched horses, he spun each freely then raised each boot toe, one at a time, and wiped the top on the fabric of his denims covering the calves of his legs. Right to left and left to right. He pulled back the blanket to stroll across the shop floor with the rowels singing as he walked.

If anyone asked where he was when the bank was robbed, he would say he was soaking down at the Barbershop.

As he left, he momentarily held the door ajar for another customer to rush past.

"Hey, Joe. Did ya hear the bank was robbed?" the man asked the Barber.

His back to the Barbershop, the man smirked at the question as he ambled away ready to enjoy his day. Overly satisfied with himself he headed for the rooming house to relax before indulging in a game of cards at a local saloon.

"I heard the ruckus. Didn't go out, though. Fella might get shot getting into the middle of something like that," Joe answered.

On the other side of the street, Clay continued his trek down the boardwalk and into the dry goods store. He was set to get himself a new pair of pants to replace the ragged ones he now wore. Although they were clean, the cold wind blowing off the snow cut through the holes like a knife. It barely warmed by the time it hit the other side of his pants and went out the front as another bitter draft blew in through the back.

Clay puzzled over the bank robbery while he looked at the items stacked on a long table in the middle of the store.

A woman entered the store and went immediately to the counter.

"Good morning, Miss Honora," the owner greeted her. "I've got your packages the stable hand ordered right here."

He lifted several brown-paper wrapped bundles onto the counter.

"Will he be coming back to pick them up? It appears it's more than you need to carry yourself."

"No. He's busy with other things. I stopped to see how many there were on my way to the post office. It doesn't look like it will be a problem for me to get them back to the house. Perhaps you can stack them and bind them with string so I can grasp that for a handle?"

"They're bulky, not heavy. I'll do what I can. If there's more than you can manage, I'll get the livery boy down at the stable next to the hotel to bring them over."

"Thank you. I'll stop back by later, then."

"Of course."

"Hello, Honora." The owner's wife came from the back

room with her arms full of bolts of new fabric. "Will Mr. O'Flannery be joining the family for Christmas?"

"No. Unfortunately, he is away on business."

"That's too bad. I'm sure the children will miss him."

With exuberance Honora replied, "But, we do have Miss Holly home for the holidays! And, the Mr. ordered presents made for the children before he left."

At the mention of Holly's name, Clay's head jerked up from the pair of stiff new pants he was studying.

Holly! Holly is home!

"I'm sure she'll be excited to see the children open their presents," the wife replied as her husband approached Clay.

"Can I help you select a pair of pants," he asked.

Clay fumbled with the metal button on a waistband. His fingers shook with excitement at the unintentional news.

"Uh, do you have any that are heavier material? The weather hasn't been too good lately."

"Of course. There's some made from thicker canvas on that other table."

"Thanks."

The owner returned behind the counter as the woman called Honora left the building.

"Did you hear that, Samuel? Ol' man O'Flannery paid somebody to make the kids presents instead of buying them from us. You'd think, as much money as he's got, he could spread some of it around to his neighbors a little better. And, you'd think he could put off his "business" until after the holidays to be with his kids."

"Shhhh. None of our business, Martha," he whispered to his wife as he nodded to the fact that they had a customer in the building.

"Well, I'd hate to think you'd treat us that way. If'n you ever got rich," Martha shot back as if to say, "Not much chance of that!"

She moved around the counter and dropped more bolts of cloth loudly onto a table. She picked up each bolt of material and arranged it roughly next to similar materials.

It was clear to Clay that Ian's new-found wealth was a sore spot for some people in the settlement, especially the owners of the main mercantile.

He didn't let himself dwell on that issue long. He was more interested in the fact that Holly was here in the same place he was. He wanted to know if she was married, but dared not ask the owner's wife who, apparently, liked to gossip.

He picked out a pair of the heaviest pants he could find and went to the counter to pay for them. The bundles awaiting pickup were still sitting on top of the rough-built counter.

He'd like to offer to deliver them, but thought better of that. What if Holly was angry with him. What would she say when he showed up at her door unannounced with his arms full of their packages? Ian was nothing to worry about since he was "away on business."

But, he was sure he had hurt Holly enough by disappearing on her. It had been too long, now, to go back and try to explain. He felt his heart sink. He would have to finish the day out at the hotel where he would put on his new pants and have supper before turning in for a good night's sleep in preparation to head out of town early Christmas morning.

No, Holly was not to be in his life. He couldn't expect her to be. Time changes all things. Especially the way one person feels about another. I best leave her in peace and go on my way, he decided as he walked back to the hotel. As for the good night's sleep, he doubted that would happen either. Especially not with him knowing he was so close to Holly yet so far apart from her. The walls of the O'Flannery estate sealed her inside like a fortress and, with someone else to run errands and do chores, there would be no cause for her to be outside those walls.

"Say," he turned back to the owner before he opened the door to leave, "is there a Christmas Eve service at the church tonight?"

"Of course. There always is. Six o'clock so folks can get back and have time with their families afterward."

"Thanks," Clay said remembering it was a given that the small white, structure with the tall steeple that served as a bell tower would be packed with worshipers on the eve of the Savior's birth.

He went outside with his package under his arm and walked down the boardwalk to the hotel.

Later that evening as he lay on his bed in his thick new blue Levis in the darkened room he heard the church bell toll.

He raised himself up to sit on the edge of the bed wanting to answer its call but, reluctantly, staying put.

No, his conscience told him. It wouldn't be good to show himself in the crowd. If someone recognized him, it could mean trouble. If Holly recognized him, he didn't know how to explain his absence in public.

Instead, he lay back down and struggled to figure out how he was going to ever straighten his life out. *Maybe it would have been better if he had stayed in Montana,* he told himself.

He faintly heard the voices singing Christmas carols in the church as the sound wafted its way through the town's atmosphere.

~*~

Once the program was over inside the church, children rushed about to pick up their small brown paper sacks containing an orange, a few nuts and some hard candy from

83

the front of the room.

It was a bitter sweet moment for Holly, who sat in the back row watching as Amy and Bradley accepted their gift. Seeing the children so excited about receiving the small bags containing candy and an orange took her mind back to the last Christmas Eve when Clay kissed her.

She remembered the Christmas morning when the children received a similar gift that he had so generously left for them. She shook the memories away and sought out the minister. She spoke quietly to him.

"It was a beautiful service, Pastor. And, the Christmas tree is lovely."

"Thank you, Miss O'Flannery. I gather you and your family are well and happy this holiday season."

"Yes. Thank you for asking. I'll be going back to school soon, though." A cloud of sadness crossed her face. "But, here, I wanted to give you something to help buy food for those who don't have a Christmas dinner for their table." She secretly slipped some money into his palm so none of the other parishioners would notice.

"It was wonderful seeing the joy on all the children's faces when they received their treats," the preacher said. "I do appreciate your seeing to it that that happens. Your generosity is beyond what anyone could expect."

"Holly! Holly! Holly!" Amy jumped up and down by her side. "Did you see the tree? Look what was in our bags!"

Bradley hurried to her side but waited patiently.

"Yes! Thank the reverend and we must go. The weather is getting colder and we didn't bring the carriage."

"Bless you, Holly," the preacher said as she moved to usher the children out of the church. "Although the store is closed now, I'm sure Samuel will let me in later this evening to gather some very welcome items to distribute to the local poor families."

~*~

Clay looked out the window of his darkened room. He saw light glowing from the open church door. The first to exit the church were the figures of a woman and two young children. They moved from the warmth of the sanctuary and headed down the darkened road. The shape of a boy hung back with the woman while the smaller child that appeared to be a girl skipped ahead kicking clumps of left-over snow with the toes of her boots in the dim light a few windows threw across the mud.

The people disappeared around a corner. When he could no longer see them, he dropped the curtain and got into bed.

CHAPTER EIGHT

The next morning the sound of the church bells ringing joyously roused him from his disturbed sleep. It was Christmas Day and time for celebration.

Clay gathered his saddlebags and checked out with the clerk.

After yesterday's run-in with the fellow in the rawhide jacket, he decided it would be best to find breakfast elsewhere rather than chance entering the dining room.

"Sure you don't want to stay for Christmas dinner," the younger man asked.

"No. I've got to be getting down the road," Clay replied.

"Do you have family waiting somewhere?" The clerk appeared curious as to what would drive a man out into the blustery Christmas morning without so much as a meal.

"Yeah, I promised someone I'd make it in before nightfall," Clay lied. He hadn't really promised anything. It was a dream of his to return to the Collier Ranch. He'd heard Mrs. Collier didn't believe the rumors and had, in fact, tried to squelch them as best she could.

"Clay wouldn't harm the Captain," she insisted

whenever the subject came up. "They're wrong. That's all. Just plain wrong. When the Captain didn't get home when we expected, I asked Clay to go look for him. It had to be a case of mistaken identity. Clay is a good boy. He's like one of our own!" A concerned expression crossed her face.

But there were a few men in town who wouldn't listen, declaring his guilt to anyone who would hear them out.

"I'll pick my horse up in an hour or so," he promised. "Got an errand to run first."

The clerk nodded. As far as he was concerned Clay was paid up until afternoon. There was not much chance of renting the room or stable space to anyone traveling on Christmas Day.

Clay removed his money from his saddle bags. Leaving only his extra clothes inside, he hung them in the stall with his horse. He checked the animal's condition and, finding it good, went to see if the saloon served breakfast as well as alcohol on the holiday.

If not, surely, there would be someplace that served food even on the most sacred holiday of the year, he reasoned.

As he approached the largest building he could hear music coming from a piano. The tune was muted and melancholy as though the player missed a life left behind.

Clay stepped through the door and approached the bar. He ordered the food available for the day and a cup of coffee. The man behind the counter filled a plate with what appeared to be some type of foul and mashed potatoes and gravy heaped high to the side. A slab of bread balanced on the top. He took his plate and found a place to sit and eat at a nearby table.

It certainly wasn't breakfast as one would consider it. But, Clay was willing to accept whatever was available rather than sit face-to-face with the man at the hotel that was trying to figure out where he had seen him before.

Or to run into Holly when he was unprepared. He judged that Christmas morning church services were still underway so he had no fear of that. An emptiness wedged in his chest as he reluctantly accepted the fact that he would be riding out without seeing her. Perhaps he would never have another opportunity to come this way again. He felt that the chapter of his life which he treasured that held Holly so dear to him was about to end.

Now, who's melancholy, he questioned himself as the piano player set the instrument to continue playing from punched paper rolls without his fingers on the keys.

Clay finished his meal and strode back to the livery stable shortly before noon. Having decided not to allow himself to see Holly, or be seen by her, he figured the best thing he could do, until he could clear his name, was ride out now. He saddled up the horse and slung his saddle bags into place. Once outside and mounted, he headed toward the Carson River ranch he had once called home.

Ahead, as he moved toward a small hill where no buildings stood. He saw three figures at a higher elevation than where he sat astride Buckshot.

He reined his horse in to watch the activity. It looked like a fun day on a snowy slope and, though he wasn't participating, he well remembered the thrill of a fast ride down a hill in the wintertime.

They appeared to be the same people he had seen the night before exiting the church. One person was twice as tall as the two smaller-bodied people. She was obviously a woman, Clay could tell by the cloak she wore with a hood pulled over her head. Covered like that, Clay could not make out her features. The two smaller figures buzzed about like a couple of bees. Finally, the woman bent and situated the smallest child in a sled shaped like a swan. The other child waited patiently nearby as he, too, prepared to slide to the base of the knoll.

One figure, a boy it appeared, flopped on his belly onto a flat sled and rode the brief ride to the bottom of the hill. He stood up and pulled the sled by its rope to the side until he was out of the way of the smaller child's path.

Soon, the swan with the child inside followed the route the sled's rails had made on the downhill slope.

Clay heard the youngster's calls of joy as the swan sped toward the bottom where he anticipated it would stop. Her squeals of excitement turned to shrieks of fear momentarily.

The woman screamed and ran down the slope after the swan. Clay saw, now, that the contraption continued on until it slowly disappeared at the base of the hill.

Something was terribly wrong!

Quickly, he raced his horse off the road and toward the frantic sounds of a woman screaming.

"Hold on, Amy! I'm coming!" The woman's voice came back to him as she called reassurance to the child.

As he drew closer to the crest of the hill he saw a pond, frozen now except for the spot where the swan had crashed through its thin coat of ice leaving a fractured hole in its surface.

The white-painted swan, with its etched feathers on its wooden wings snug against its sides, sunk quickly. Only the yellow beak at the end of the head on its long curved neck was visible.

Then, nothing.

"Amy! Bradley, help quickly," the woman called to the boy as she ran toward the pond.

To her dismay, she, too, saw the sled sinking beneath the ice as she stumbled over the snow and bushes toward the little girl.

Before she reached the pond, Clay dismounted on the

run while Buckshot skidded to a halt.

Clay jumped into the water sinking up to his knees in mud at first. Then, upon reaching the crash site, dropped below the water completely. Frantically, as he swam, he ran his hands through the icy water and chunks of splintered ice.

On shore, the woman sunk to her knees sobbing and calling the girl's name over and over.

"Amy! Amy!"

So intent was she on seeing the child come to the surface she paid no attention to the stranger that searched for her sister. The small boy, Bradley, stood on the bank near the edge of the ice and unashamedly let tears fall down his wind-whipped reddened cheeks.

At last Clay pulled the small child's body up from the murky water and surfaced with her in his arms.

Laying limp within his grasp, with legs and arms dangling, Amy didn't flex a muscle.

"Oh, God! Oh, God!" The woman moaned.

The boy stumbled toward her and dropped to her side. The rope of his own sled was clutched tightly in one fist as he kneeled helplessly next to the woman.

On land, Clay laid the girl on the ground and began to try to work the icy water out of the child's lungs. He moved her arms up and pressed carefully on her chest. Then, he turned her over and tried pushing on her back below her shoulder blades.

The woman rocked on her knees praying and not wanting to interfere in his rescue efforts.

She stared at Clay, her eyes questioning his when he looked up.

Clay shook his head but gave orders.

"Go to my saddle bags and get my dry clothes to wrap her in." It would keep the distraught woman busy momentarily even if the rescue attempt was hopeless.

As he spoke, he continued to put pressure on the girl's back in an attempt to force the water out and air back into her lungs. He tried desperately to bring the child back although he was losing hope with every passing second.

At last, he heard a slight whine. Water sprayed from the child's mouth. She choked and coughed. Suddenly, Amy popped her eyes open.

Thank God! Clay thought. *I couldn't have stood for her to die and cause more pain for Holly. And, it was Holly,* he knew as soon as he stood facing her with Amy in his arms.

"Holly!" Amy shrieked, frightened by her experience and waking up with a stranger leaning over her.

Holly wrapped Clay's warm, dry shirt around Amy.

"We better get her home and into a hot bath," Holly said, calm, now that the emergency was over and Amy was alive. Now it was as if she were coping with an everyday occurrence.

Her mind was minutely distracted by the fact that the man before her who saved her sister was Clay. He was older, more mature appearing, but he was Clay Bingham she was sure.

She knew it the minute they locked eyes.

"We aren't far from your house. I'll put the three of you on the horse and lead him back there," Clay said.

Clay helped Holly get into the saddle, then handed Amy up to her before helping Bradley up behind. He took his lariat from the saddle horn and tied one end to the rope on Bradley's sled. He left the length far enough behind not to interfere with Buckshot's stride. He wrapped the loose end around his shoulder as they started out.

"Thank God you came along," Holly whispered hoarsely. Her mind kept telling her perhaps she made a mistake in thinking this stranger was familiar. *Is it simply that I want him so badly to be Clay that my judgment is clouded? Am I imagining it is him?* She wondered as she studied the back of his hat as he walked alongside the horse in wet, bone-chilling clothes.

She saw steam rise from his coat back across his broad shoulders. She wished she had something warm to offer him to wrap around himself and hold his body heat in.

Not being able to help Clay, she pulled her skirt around from where it flapped against her leg and wrapped Amy tighter in another layer of cloth.

The settlement came into view. Without having to tell him, Holly realized Clay was moving toward the house enclosure and warmth. He reached for the gate latch and walked the horse up the path to the side door beneath the porch roof.

Lifting Bradley to the ground, he spoke to the boy.

"Would you go inside and ask someone to fill a tub with warm water for the little one?"

"Please," He added remembering not to throw orders into the air to the child without softening the tone of his command. He reached to take Amy from Holly's arms and left Holly to swing off the horse on her own as he carried the child into the house.

Amy whimpered.

"I'm cold, Holly," she fussed and Clay felt her shiver in his arms.

"You're home now. We're almost there," he said to comfort her. "We'll get you warmed up soon."

Holly ran past Clay into the house where she turned toward another room while Clay stopped in front of the fireplace. He sat the child on the rug where the heat radiated outward to thaw them both.

"As soon as I get her in the bath, I'll find you something dry to wear," Holly promised from somewhere near the back of the large room.

"Bradley, will you look for Honora? Ask her if she has the soup pot going on the stove. These two need some warm food inside them. We all do!"

She had forgotten about her own discomfort in her concern for Amy. And, although Bradley didn't complain, she quickly realized he was probably chilled, too, as well as frightened by the day's events.

Clay heard the water running and realized the O'Flannery house must be the only one around to have a first-of-its-kind system of running water. Or, he decided, at least hot water. Turning to warm his backside, he thought how much more convenient inside utilities must be over the copper tub he had rented for a half-hour in the back of the Barbershop. A shiver shook him as the warmth from the fire fought the chill off.

Holly approached.

"I'll take her now and put her in the tub," she told Clay and gathered the child up from the floor where she sat like a little frozen statue to carry her to the bath.

Once Amy was undressed, Holly slipped her into the warm water over her whimpering protests.

"Don't like water no more!"

"I know. I don't blame you. But this is a good thing. Not like the water in the pond. See, it is shallow." Holly stirred waves in the water with her hand. "You don't need to be afraid. I'm sure you'll get comfortable with it as you relax and get cleaned up," Holly told her.

"You can soak a bit while you warm up. I'll be back in a minute to wash your hair and get the mud off you. Papa will be so angry when he finds out I let you use your new sled and it ended up in the Spangles' pond." she said more to herself than the child. "I'm so sorry, Honey. I was frightened for you!"

The younger girl, who had mostly maintained her

composure until then, started to cry again.

"No, no. Don't cry, now, Honey. It's all over. Everything is all right now. You're fine. You don't have your sled anymore but the important thing is that we have you!"

"Don't want the old sled. It's awful! The swan was supposed to swim. Other swans do. Why didn't my swan swim, Holly?"

"I don't know, Honey. Maybe it was too heavy. I'm sure if a real swan was too fat, it would have trouble staying afloat, too. You just sit there and enjoy the warm water and make sure to thank the man that helped us when you get through. OK?"

"Jimmy Spangles can have the old swan, if he wants it. I don't want it no more!"

Holly thought about how hard Amy had wished for the swan sled only a few days ago.

She remembered how her father, who usually seemed so distant, had assured the child Santa Claus would know that the swan was the only thing she asked for.

Only Holly and her father knew he had gone to the local cabinetmaker on one of his rare sober days and arranged for the swan to be constructed. It was built to be used as a sled. It was to be an enclosure that would hold the little girl safe and warm inside when someone pulled the rope. The swan was not designed to float.

Holly thought about how excited Amy had been earlier this Christmas morning before church. During the service Amy had pleaded to be taken to where she could ride the swan down a hill. Holly had shushed her, promising to see what she could do once they were back home.

Holly became overcome with the reality of Amy's near drowning and moved quickly through a second door into the adjoining bedroom. There, she felt her knees go weak with relief and the after effects of the calamity. She collapsed in muffled sobs.

Clay wondered what was taking Holly so long to return. He had heard the water shut off.

He could, now, hear the child splashing about in the tub. But heard no sound of Holly's returning footsteps.

At last, Holly crept back into the room where he sat before the fire. She had removed her wet and muddy clothes and changed into a neatly pressed dress and wore only stockings on her feet.

She sat down on the hearth rug beside him and handed him dry clothes.

"They may not fit too well. They were some my father bought. The pants legs were too long and the waist band too tight around his waist. He never got around to taking them back for a better fitting size."

Clay studied her face and saw blotchy red spots where the resultant rash from crying still showed around her eyes, although faded.

"I'm sure they'll be better than these I'm wearing now," he said to avoid embarrassment for her at recognizing the signs.

"Yours look new," Holly commented.

"They are," Clay chuckled as the feeling of relief that the disaster had not ended in the child's death flooded over him as well. He was near the same stage, emotionally, as Holly had been a few minutes ago but fought to keep control. He didn't want to show his own hysteria at what might have been. He could tell by the red around her eyelids and the tears still brimmed at the edges that she still struggled to contain herself. *It wouldn't do for him to send her emotions spinning out of control again.*

"Everything's all right, now, Holly," Clay spoke quietly as he tried to soothe her reaction to the event.

"I know. But, it was so close. So close." She shook her

head. "I guess I'm reacting with relief."

Honora entered the room with a look of concern on her face.

"What is it Miss Holly? Bradley is in the kitchen shaking at the table. What happened?"

"Honora, this is Clay Bingham. If it weren't for him Amy would most likely be drowned," Holly stated matter-of-factly.

Clay glanced at Holly having forgotten his wish to be unrecognized with the unfolding crisis still fresh in his mind. Obviously, he hadn't changed enough to fool her.

Honora gasped and crossed herself.

"Madre Mia! What has happened?"

"I'll explain later. The good news is she is fine now. I have to go get her out of the tub."

"Your brother asked about soup. There is food ready in the kitchen." Honora offered what assistance she could.

"Good. I'll get Amy dried off and dressed. Then Clay can go change his clothes and we'll all have something hot to warm us while we wait for Christmas dinner to finish cooking. Perhaps I'll have a cup of tea, if you would put the kettle on for me, Honora."

With her words Clay realized there was an aroma in the house of roasting turkey and a blend of other pleasant smells. He recognized the fragrance of cinnamon, nutmeg, and ginger used to flavor apple and pumpkin pies, that fairly saturated the air.

"Clay will be staying for dinner," Holly told Honora without consulting him.

He looked at her inquiringly. *Was that so wise with the way her father felt?* He wondered.

"Are you sure?"

"Of course I'm sure. Honora, please set another place for Clay at the dining room table."

"Yes, Miss Holly. It will be a pleasure." Honora muttered to herself in Spanish as she left the room.

"She is saying a prayer of thanksgiving," Holly told him. "She is very grateful to you, too."

Holly returned to where Amy was becoming bored with her bath. She wrapped her in a large towel and carried her into the adjoining bedroom and shut the door.

"The room's all yours, Clay," she called to him. "Leave your dirty clothes there and I'll have Honora get them washed."

"That's not necessary."

"I'm more than happy to take care of the damage we've created."

Clay cautiously poked his head into the room where a large tub sat. He heard the muddy water draining slowly.

Quickly he changed into the clothes Holly had supplied. The pants were too long for him, as well, and the waist slid down without a belt. He bent over and turned the material on the pants legs up into a cuff so he could walk without tripping.

Holly had included a pair of wool socks in the stack of clothes for him.

Dressed in dry clothes, he returned to set his boots near the fireplace hoping the warmth would remove some of the moisture and they would be mostly dry before he had to leave.

All the while, he wondered what he did next. He felt like his mind was spinning. He wondered what Holly thought about his sudden appearance. Would she consider him a stranger she didn't really know? Would she talk rationally with him or tell him to leave once she felt she completed her obligation for Amy's rescue?

Amy padded out in stocking feet and, studying Clay gratefully, headed for the kitchen.

Holly followed close behind.

Suddenly, things felt awkward to Clay.

"I really should be going," he told Holly.

"Nonsense! This family is indebted to you! No matter what others might think, I don't believe the gossip. And, I won't let anyone say anything bad about you. They have to know that you saved Amy's life."

"Really, I'm sure anyone would have done their best to save her — "

"No one else was there, Clay. Now, you must have a bite to eat. I insist."

"My horse is still standing out in the storm. I should go get him under shelter." Clay tried to find a way to avoid what might turn out to be a progressively more awkward situation, if he stayed.

"After we get something warm inside us, I'll send Bradley for the stable hand. He can unsaddle your horse and put him up in our stable."

"We'll have Christmas dinner and then I'll show you to your room."

"But, I can't stay here. Maybe I can still get a room at the hotel."

"No," Holly insisted. "We have plenty of room. My father is gone and I will not turn you out in this weather for any reason!"

Over Clay's protests it was plain to see that Holly would not relent. He sensed she was a much stronger woman, now, than she had been as a girl.

It was becoming clear to Clay that Holly was not about to let him off the hook. He had left her once. While she had surely figured out what prompted that departure, he had a feeling she was going to get around to demanding more details. He was sure she would not let him leave again without knowing the full story.

This was not the same timid Holly he had known three years ago. She was a more confident, determined young woman. She had not only grown in physical stature, but in mental strength as well. Somehow, he felt he had met his match.

CHAPTER NINE

Having blended back into the local population, the man with the rawhide jacket now left the coat behind in his room when he ventured out in public. Finding that a piece of the fringe had been torn from its edge, he decided to take no further risks by wearing the coat. He wasn't sure where he might have lost the scrap of rawhide. But, there were several places it may have dropped that could cause trouble for him.

Chances were good it fell into the mud of the road or on the trail, but the risk of wearing something that stood out so much was more, now, than he wanted to take.

At his first opportunity he went to the general store where he purchased a heavy canvas coat with ticking between the outside and the inner lining.

It was not nearly as classy as his other coat but serviceable and warm, he decided.

Back in his room he shaved in tepid water although the razor tugged the whiskers roughly.

His mustache and beard were gone. His sideburns were shortened.

If anyone had gotten a look at him at the bank, he felt they would be doubtful it was him when they saw him now.

Brazen enough, he took his breakfast the next morning with the banker.

As they sat chewing their food and drinking their coffee he thought carefully about his words before he spoke them.

He studied Tyler Washington as he finished his meal watching him tip his cup and drain the remainder of the coffee into his mouth.

"Real sorry to hear your bank got robbed."

Tyler Washington grunted.

"I can understand you might not want to talk about it."

"No point. The guy got the money and nobody knew who he was."

"Wonder where our breakfast partner that was here the other day went to?"

Tyler Washington's expression perked up.

"Not that I'm sayin' he might a done it, o' course."

"No. No, but you've got a point. He did disappear rather quickly."

"I'as suspicious o' him from the get-go. Never gave us a name. I know him from somewhere. But, just can't put a finger on it."

"Well, nobody got a good look at the robber anyway," Tyler Washington said with resignation.

"I'm sure the Sheriff will do his best to figure out who it was. Mark my words, you'll know what I'm sayin' when they find him."

"I'll give the Sheriff your tip. I'm sure he'll look for him."

The man nodded his head. He rose to set his dishes on the sideboard. With his back to the banker as he left, he let a smirk twist his thin lips.

With any luck, he had deflected any possible suspicion from himself onto the missing hotel guest.

CHAPTER TEN

In his office early the morning after the Christmas holiday, the Sheriff fingered the small piece of light tan rawhide as he sat with his feet propped on his desktop. The heel of his boot, where one foot crossed over the other, kept his chair well balanced while he tilted back and puzzled over the fragment.

Someone must have seen the larger section of cowhide this came off of, he thought as possibilities ran through his mind. *Crappy clue I got here. Not much to go on.*

But, it was all he had.

"Like lookin' for a needle in a haystack," his wife would say. And, he couldn't disagree.

He flicked the material with his thumbnail. It landed on top of his desk and he studied it further without adjusting his chair or taking his feet down.

There was no point in dragging a posse out again with the trail gone cold. No reason to hurry as he had more pressing things to do. Not to say the least of which included finding the murderer of Captain Collier a few years back. A case that had sat too long on his desk and gone cold.

The one suspect had hightailed it out of town and, for all he knew, out of the country.

Clay Bingham had been the only one that the scant evidence pointed to at the time. Bingham, when the Captain had been killed, was a very young man who would never have been glanced at with suspicion had it not been for the accusations pointed in his direction by the drunken members of a mob.

He pondered the night the mob became unruly. He dreaded that the man had escaped before he'd had a chance to question him. But, then, at the time he had wanted no vigilante hanging, either.

His list of unsolved crimes was stacking up on his desk. If he didn't start showing some action on them, he feared his job might be in jeopardy when the next election came around.

One thing the people wanted was action when it came to killings and thievery.

Although bank robbery was a serious crime, the Sheriff felt Captain Collier's murder topped the list, as cold as that trail might be.

The Sheriff straightened up, moved his feet to the floor and shoved his chair back. He reached for his hat and duster. He stuffed the small piece of rawhide into his pants pocket before opening the door to walk a slow patrol in front of the buildings.

Where could he start his search? It seemed futile and a waste of effort on his part.

Early in the morning, the boardwalks were empty and only the hollow sound his own boots made on the wood echoed back at him. Few storekeepers stirred but small wisps of smoke came from chimneys as fires were built and people began to start their day. Only the hotel appeared to have activity in it and he smelled the aroma of strong coffee along with smoke as wind-fallen dry cottonwood blazed inside the cook stove emitting the scent in a larger plume of smoke than he'd like to see from the hotel chimneys.

"Damn! I've told the Swansons not to go building such hot fires. I suppose they've got the fireplace rip-roaring along, too!" He spoke out loud as he glanced at the third chimney at the side of the building. *Sure enough, there's smoke there too. One of these days one of 'em's going to set the whole place ablaze!*

He hurried toward the hotel to warn the proprietors once more.

Shouldn't be my job to have to look after these easterners that come here and don't know how different things are. Especially in the depth of winter. The building's so dried out by the winds and lack of moisture it could flare up without a minute's notice. Not much safer now than midsummer when the outside heat only adds to the extreme fire danger.

Sometimes, it seemed to him, his job was more trouble than it was worth. But, he hung in there to support himself and his wife, knowing there wasn't much other work he could do that would keep him close to home.

As he reached for the door knob, two men and Mrs. Swanson burst through toward him.

"Fire!" Mrs. Swanson shouted. "Fire!"

"Grab a bucket," Mr. Washington called out. "I'll break the ice on the horse trough!"

While Mrs. Swanson scurried around like a hen outside its pen not knowing where to go, the other man rushed away.

"I'll see if I can find another bucket," he called back over his shoulder as he ran in the opposite direction.

"Hurry! Hurry!" Mrs. Swanson shouted to the men as the fire ignited more and more of the building.

Sheriff Jamison burst into action, grabbing a fire bucket from its nail on the building next to the hotel.

Mrs. Swanson clutched another and tossed it to Mr. Washington who, now, had chunks of ice floating on top of the scant amount of water.

"We're going to need more water than this! Sound the alarm! Run for the fire department. Get help!"

Heeding his words, Mrs. Swanson ran screaming "Fire!" as loud as she could shout the couple of blocks it took to reach the building where a hand-pump cart sat outside. By the time she arrived, men were already grabbing the long side poles that normally would be hitched to a horse and dragging the cart toward the hotel which was, quickly, an inferno.

The calm of the town's day after Christmas was broken.

In all the confusion no one noticed that the other hotel guest never returned with an additional bucket.

CHAPTER ELEVEN

"Did you hear the ruckus early this morning?" Holly asked her houseguest during a late breakfast after the hotel fire. "Bradley's been pestering me about the fire ever since he got up! I told him I didn't have any information for him."

Clay had retired to his room the night before when she signaled it was time to end the evening and quiet the house.

Although he was an early riser, he had lain stretched out on the bed long before sun rise. It was as dark as midnight while he laid in the unlit room waiting for day to break. With the room on the side of the house that faced the central buildings of town, the glow from the fire threw a false sun rise across the window. With Holly's room on the other side of the hall, Clay was sure she was oblivious to anything that was going on at the other buildings.

Clay arose and, never having drawn the heavy curtains across the glass, he lifted the light lace panel and tried to detect which building was burning.

With the O'Flannery house isolated on its acreage a distance away from the main wooden buildings and no heavy wind, he reasoned they were safe.

Now, breakfast was being served and Holly, tired of Bradley's incessant questions about the activity outside, sought Clay's input to give her time to eat.

"Joshua said it might burn down everything," Bradley announced excitedly. "Wish you'd woke me up early, Holly. I'd like to have seen the big fire. It's mostly gone now."

"Whatever it was, it was a good distance away from us. You needn't worry."

"Yes," Clay answered Holly's question. "The glow through the window got my attention, too. I could see the flames but wasn't sure just which building was involved."

"The hotel! Joshua said," Bradley informed him.

Holly shook her head. "Joshua picked up some hay at the livery early this morning. He helped what he could but it was mostly under control by the time he got there. Everybody is talking about the fire, he said. I guess he had to excite Bradley with it, too."

"Nothing wrong with a little excitement — as long as nobody got hurt. Buildings can be replaced," Clay said.

Then, hoping he hadn't been out of line with his comment, he stirred sugar into his coffee and lifted the cup to his lips.

Holly watched him as he sipped his coffee. She liked the way he didn't make a slurping noise when he drank, like some men she had noticed. She, also, liked that he placed the napkin over his lap. *It was good for Bradley to see men could be refined, not crude and rough all the time.*

Clay had manners. Maybe not as nice as the men back East — personally she thought them too overdone for her. Perhaps had she grown up from a young age with a rich father, she might feel differently. But, she liked a little edge to her men. She chuckled internally. The only man she had known romantically had been Clay. And then it had been with the innocence of youth. The others were just not her

107

style and, whether she had ever put loving Clay on hold or not, she couldn't say.

She simply knew he wasn't the terrible man her father and some of his drinking cronies tried to make him out to be.

"Well, anyway, Joshua said — "

"Bradley! Enough! Joshua also said the men had it mostly under control when he got there. The flames were pretty much gone and they were working on the coals in the hot spots. Now, let us eat our meal in peace, please!"

Bradley studied his food on his plate while his sister, Amy, taunted him for Holly's reprimand.

"Mind your manners, Bradley. Holly said we have a guest and we should behave ourselves."

"Sorry." Bradley said to Clay as he let his chin drop to his chest to show him he meant his words.

Not knowing how to respond, Clay nodded his head.

"Can't say as how I might not feel the same as you if I was your age," Clay found words to ease the child's concern at displeasing his sisters.

Bradley quickly turned his attention to cleaning his plate of food and asked to be excused.

Amy dropped from her chair and followed him into the playroom.

Clay imbedded the image of Holly, sitting at the opposite end of the table, into his mind.

She had grown more beautiful as she matured. Her red curly hair was piled high on top of her head and a long strand hung down from the back and fell over her left shoulder.

When she looked back at him her bright blue eyes seemed to catch the morning sunlight and sparkle.

"I am so relieved you didn't go to the hotel last night. Who knows, you might have been hurt or, worse, killed.

Joshua said the fire started so early there was concern that someone might still be asleep in one of the rooms upstairs." Then, as if to change the conversation she asked, "Do you have plans for today?"

Clay wondered if she had caught him staring at her and quickly answered her question.

"I do have an errand to do that will take me on a short trip."

"Oh! Well, will you be returning soon?"

"Soon."

"I'll ask Honora to pack you some food. Even with the sun out and shining brightly, it's bitter cold out there and you could probably use something to eat later."

She wondered where Clay's trip would take him and when he would return but tried not to pry. *After all, he did tell me he was going so it isn't likely he'll disappear like the last time,* she reassured herself.

Clay noted a look of concern on her face.

"Thank you." He studied her, thinking that she must be remembering his last disappearance from her life. "This time, no matter what, I won't leave without letting you know I'm going, Holly," he promised.

"I guess the first experience is just too raw, yet," she admitted demurely.

"I have to do some things that I hope will help clear my name."

"I understand," she said as she recalled the nasty rumors that swirled through the community when he left before.

"Besides, maybe I can find some information out for Bradley. I stayed in that hotel a couple of nights. I'd like to know what happened, too."

Holly shook her head at him in a repeat of how she had Bradley. "Don't men ever grow up? Or are they always curious little boys?" she teased.

"Doesn't the news intrigue you even a little bit?"

"Certainly not like it does Bradley! Besides, I don't think you should risk getting yourself in trouble just to satisfy his curiosity. I'm sure, in a few days, he'll forget all about it."

"You may be right. But, in the meantime, I have to work on finding out who killed Captain Collier. I have to make it known that I am an upright citizen before — " Clay let his words drop.

"Before what, Clay?"

He wanted to say, "Before we can make a life together," but changed the subject.

"Thank you for the great breakfast. Honora did a perfect job." He noted he liked the comfortable way of life even though it had been only a few short hours that he had stayed in the O'Flannery household.

When he had protested his visit at first, Holly had finally explained how she, a single woman, would justify his being in the house. "I'll just tell people we have a new boarder."

"As if they would believe that!" Clay had responded. But, he eventually gave in and now enjoyed the family interaction and pleasant meals he was sharing.

"I need to get my horse," He told Holly as he went to politely assist her from her chair.

He took her soft small palm in his and, as she lifted herself up toward him, he bent to briefly touch her lips with his.

It was a timid kiss for fear of interruption by one of the children or the housekeeper.

"I'll miss you," Clay said.

Restraining herself from throwing her body into his arms, she said, "I'll miss you too. But this isn't a final goodbye, is it?"

"No. Of course not! I will return. I promised."

Then to lighten the moment Clay added, "And I'll miss the wonderful meals. You have learned well that the way to a man's heart is through his stomach," he tossed an old quote from his recently kissed lips and smiled at her.

"Then court Honora, Sir. I have nothing to do with that, other than suggest what we might enjoy."

"This time, I will be back," he promised her quietly. *And, he thought, when I do perhaps I'll be able to ask you to marry me.*

~*~

Clay took leave of Holly's hospitality, and the warmth of her home and lips.

He found Buckshot in a stall inside the stable. The stable boy curried the horse with care and looked up as its owner approached.

"Good Morning, Sir," the boy spoke.

"Good Morning to you as well. Thank you for taking care of my horse. I'm sure he'd much rather be in here getting pampered than out where I have to take him." Clay reached for his saddle to ready Buckshot for the ride.

"Miss O'Flannery's a calling me," the boy said and sprinted off toward the house.

Just as quickly as he left, he returned with the promised bundle of food Holly sent.

"Miss O'Flannery said to tell you she'll be awaiting your return, Sir," the boy said as Clay mounted Buckshot. The boy held the flour sack up for him to tie to the saddle horn.

Clay flipped a small coin to the boy and thanked him again. He left the young one standing watching him leave as he hefted the coin in his open hand. Clay touched his hat with his finger tips.

Once settled comfortably in the saddle, he rode toward the buildings and, then, slowly past the burned out hotel without stopping. He could hear the talk of the conflagration still buzzing as the main topic of conversation between the people standing about staring in shock. There wasn't much left to tell him what started the fire. He certainly did not want to dismount and become involved in something that might lead to trouble. He considered that there was nothing he could do to help, anyway. It would be best to leave it up to the Sheriff to decide whether it was accidental or arson.

He turned Buckshot onto the trail that would lead past the pond where he found Holly and the children the day before.

Dark smoke hung heavy in the overcast sky.

He let Buckshot increase his pace as they rode through the back country toward the Collier Ranch. Buckshot slowed as the landscape became so rugged Clay was forced to give Buckshot his head and let him pick his way for a short stretch of trail. Clay listened intently and, when he heard hoof beats coming from either direction, walked his horse off the road into the nearby brush.

Upon hearing a rapidly running mount approaching him from behind, he moved Buckshot to the side of the road, across a creek and behind a large mound of dirt. The mound was not big enough to be called a hill but it was still large enough to conceal a horse and rider.

He reached forward and put his hand across the horse's nostrils — a signal for quiet from his well-trained steed. The two were statuesque and hidden.

He studied the lone rider as he rushed by.

It was the man he had seen before at the hotel and at the Barbershop. It was the fellow who had worn the new rawhide jacket that was fringed at the edge at breakfast his first morning at the hotel. It was the man he thought was following him earlier. Only, now, he was clean shaven. *Was he following his trail? Why else would he be riding in this direction? And, in such a hurry?*

Clay sat his horse and let the man get a distance ahead of him before moving back onto the road. He rode a short ways and found another trail that he knew still led to the Collier Ranch — the back way.

When Clay approached the clearing where the ranch house stood he stopped Buckshot in a clump of old cottonwoods. He dismounted and tied him where he could nibble blades of winter worn grass without being observed by anyone inside the house.

Clay crept along the edge of the outer trees growing along a running creek until he could see the house and its surrounding outbuildings from different vantage points.

He noted that the corral was empty and none of the cowboys seemed to be around. *Out on the range tending to the herd,* he presumed.

He saw the buggy parked alongside the barn and the horse that usually pulled it in the lower pasture. That told him Mrs. Collier must surely be home and probably in the house. He intended to talk to her, but not if the rider was already inside.

When he reached a spot where he could observe the side yard next to the bunkhouse he saw a horse tied to the hitching rail. He recognized it as the one the man that passed him on the trail was riding.

The horse stood sleeping, now, with one rear leg lifted and locked and his head down and eyes closed. The gelding would be of no interest if he hadn't a short time ago been galloping down the road with the stranger on his back.

Clay edged himself into a spot where he felt he could clearly see a smaller piece of the yard and get to the side of the house without being noticed.

He wasn't sure if the man was in the main house or the bunkhouse but he intended to find out which.

Stooping low enough to avoid being seen through the

kitchen window, Clay hurried to the back section of the house. He squeezed himself tight against the corner where the house and back porch joined.

Above and to the side, near where the two walls formed a corner, a small window was pushed out at the bottom a crack and he could hear people talking inside.

The tones were eerily familiar. The words were a blend of the two voices he had heard before the Captain died — only they were no longer hushed. The man was shouting and Mrs. Collier answered back in a shrieking pitch.

CHAPTER TWELVE

Later in the morning, after the fire had been fought and quelled, the smoke and fallen ash eventually cleared from the air. Nothing was left of the hotel except its stone fireplace chimney.

Everything else lay as rubble or melted metal in the still smoldering ashes. There a metal bed frame showed its rounded edges and smaller tube rails connected to the headboard. The remains were warped and grey. The second story of the hotel had collapsed onto the first so furniture and any retrievable items were mixed together.

The Sheriff came to stand outside where the hotel once was complete and serving the citizenry.

Mrs. Swanson remained starring dully into what had been her home and business. She still wore her soot-streaked dress beneath a too-big man's grey coat someone had tossed over her shoulders. She wrung her hands and fretted at the loss as tears ran down her smoke and ash covered face.

"The Mister is going to be so upset with me," she said as she stared into the still hot coals.

115

"I'm sure, when he gets back, he'll be glad you are still alive. It didn't take the livery. That's something good. Right?" The Sheriff tried to encourage the distraught woman.

"I told him, like you told me, Sheriff, not to build too big a fire. But, he wouldn't listen. Said it was too blasted cold and he didn't pay to freeze his pants off."

"Who, Mrs. Swanson?" *Surely, it wasn't Mr. Washington! He'd know better. And, Mr. Swanson, or the boy, had been nowhere around to be seen.*

"Where is your husband, anyway?"

"James and my Jimmy went off to hunt. The Mister said the snow would make tracking easier. We needed venison to feed the guests as well as ourselves. Guess that doesn't matter now — " she broke off and a heavy sob escaped her lips as if it came from the bottom of her lungs.

"What are we goin' to do?"

Not wanting to discourage the woman any further the Sheriff spoke gently, "Well, I recon' you'll have to find another building to set up a hotel in until you can rebuild. Mr. Washington needs some place to stay. Maybe he can give you folks a loan to get you back in business."

The woman looked dismayed and shook her head. "I don't know. Don't know how much credit we'd be able to get."

The Sheriff reminded her, again, about his question, "Who built the fires, Mrs. Swanson?"

"Well, with the Mister off, one of the guests said he'd do it. I told him not to put too much kindling in and only a small amount of the paper-dry wood. But, he must not have listened... "

"How many guests did you have?"

"Two, Mr. Washington and a man named Everett Simmons. Mr. Simmons was the one who built the fires."

"Everett Simmons," the Sheriff searched his memory for the name. "Know anything about him? Where he came from? What he does for a living?"

"No. He's a very quiet man. Only, him and Mr. Washington talked sometimes at breakfast."

It occurred to the Sheriff, as she spoke, that the clean-shaven "Mr. Simmons" had somehow left the scene of the fire and not returned. He had not seen him assisting in anyway to put out the destructive fire he had started, be it accidentally because of stubbornness or — ? But, what other reason would he have. *It must have been ignorance*, the Sheriff decided. But, he made a mental note to talk to Tyler Washington as soon as he could.

Washington had gone to rest on a settee in his office at the bank after commandeering one of his off-duty teller's jackets to cover Mrs. Swanson from the chill of the early morning air. Although the fire was often blistering hot to their skin as they faced it, their backs felt the severe cold. None dared to turn their backs to the fire for warmth. They knew it was simply too dangerous to be so close or not be watchful of its flares and possible explosive eruptions.

Fortunately, the conflagration was contained to the one structure. Other nearby buildings miraculously still stood. They were scorched and what paint remained was blistered and discolored.

It was only because it was a still morning with the normal winter gusts of wind absent from the area that more people weren't facing the same losses as Mrs. Swanson did.

"You best get some rest," the Sheriff told Mrs. Swanson as a woman approached to offer a respite to her. Only an hour ago her husband had informed the Sheriff that, when the fire was under control, he'd go home and send his wife back to take Mrs. Swanson in.

The long hours of concern and hard work had taken its

toll on the hotel proprietor and she didn't hesitate to accept the offer.

"You best get some rest, too, Sheriff," Mrs. Swanson told him. "And, thank you for your help." She stood wringing her hands together as she hesitated to leave the scene.

The Sheriff nodded. *He would,* he thought, *but first he had to assign someone to watch the remnants of the hotel until the ashes could cool enough for him to get back and search through the rubble.*

He didn't know what he expected to find, if anything. But, something just didn't seem right to him. He continued to wonder about the man that seemed to have run away. Was the fire a diversion for this Mr. Simmons to disappear like he did? And why would he want to vanish, if he had? He'd have to put a search out through town for the man. He wanted to know why he didn't stay to help when he said he'd get a bucket to do so.

Sometimes he simply could not figure out the actions of people.

Why would a guest of the hotel offer to light the morning fires anyway? What namby-pamby man couldn't take a little cold? Why would he be so anxious to build a roaring fire?

CHAPTER THIRTEEN

After a hot tub bath Mrs. Swanson slept soundly for a solid nine hours, Sheriff Jamison caught little more than forty winks.

He assigned the chore of searching for Mr. Simmons to one of his deputies and told the other, "Don't let anyone disturb me." Then he dropped, exhausted, onto a crudely-made wooden cot in one of the empty jail cells.

At his home, his wife awaited his arrival knowing he wouldn't stay down long. She fixed a hot meal for him and kept it warm on the back of the stove. Occasionally, she had one of their nephews check on the possibility of his being awake.

Instead of entering the Sheriff's Office, the boy merely peered in through the dirty four-paned glass window near the Sheriff's desk where the deputy now sat.

Each time, the deputy shook his head quickly to keep the boy from entering and creating any noise.

Once, when the deputy stepped outside for a moment, the boy approached him to ask, "Ain't Uncle Charlie up yet?" This after only three hours.

119

"Recon' he'll be up soon. You run on back and tell your Aunt she can bring him some clean clothes and food when he does. Tell you what. You watch the office door and I'll stick a pillow tick over the doorknob when he wakes up."

"Yes, Sir!" The boy tore off down the street avoiding ice-crusted berms of dirt to keep from getting his boots filthy.

When the deputy heard the creak of the rough cot as the Sheriff stirred, he did as he had promised the boy, knowing it wouldn't be long before the man got up. He had learned, over the years, the habits of his boss.

He also knew Charlie would be hungry and wanting to shed the smoke-filled clothes after he washed up and before he ate.

"Afternoon, Deputy," the Sheriff's wife spoke quietly when she entered the room. She carried a folded shirt and pants over her arm and a heavy coat slung beneath them. "Recon' Charlie's about up. You know he'll want something hot to eat. That coffee you got brewing on the stove smells like it's fit to take paint off the desk your at. He'll need a descent meal to cushion his stomach against that brew."

The deputy chuckled.

The boy now stood behind Mrs. Jamison cradling a large covered bowl in his arms. A flour sack was gripped tight in his clenched fist.

"I made sure there were fresh biscuits and heated up yesterday's leftover pot roast into a stew so's he'd have something better to put in his stomach than that coffee you two drink."

"Yes, Ma'am," the deputy said as the Sheriff came from the back hall rubbing the soot that still remained, after a quick wash, from his face with a grayed towel.

"There's plenty here for you, too," Mrs. Jamison assured the deputy.

She looked at her husband then handed him the clothes

to change into. He nodded his appreciation and turned back to the wash area to slip out of the dirty clothes and into the clean ones.

While he did, Mrs. Jamison took the large bowl from the boy and sat it on the desk.

"Suppose you got a couple of bowls somewhere to match those beat up coffee cups, Deputy," she commented.

"Yes, 'm." He moved to gather a couple of chipped crockery bowls and two bent spoons.

"Land sakes! I wish you two would toss those things out and take a couple of decent pieces from my kitchen. Every time I see those things I can't help but think you're both going to die of some horrid disease."

"We're careful not to use the ones that are split down the inside, Ma'am. Don't figure these little chips on the outside rim can hurt us much. I promise, if they get chips inside, I'll make target practice out of 'em."

Mrs. Jamison nodded her approval at that. She took two rolled up squares of white cloth out of the flour sack and unwrapped clean silverware. "Keep these and, next time I come by, I'll bring you some of my stoneware. No more often then Charlie gets home on time for a meal, we won't miss them."

After a visit with his wife and nephew, the Sheriff bid them farewell. He left his office on a full stomach and wandered back down to the scene of the destruction.

"Howdy, Bill," the Sheriff greeted the deputy on guard at the scene.

"Howdy, Sheriff." Bill studied his boss as he squatted down to feel the ashes. They were still warm to his palm but not too hot that they burned his skin.

"What you doing back out here already, Charlie?"

"The Mrs. brought some stew and biscuits into the office, if you're hungry. You can take a break and come back when you're through eating. She was getting ready to clear things up when I left."

"You sure you don't want me to stay and keep the curious folks back?" The deputy asked, then came closer to the Sheriff and whispered, "What you lookin' for Sheriff? Somebody die in the fire?"

"Not near as we could tell. I'm not sure what I expect to find." The Sheriff stuffed his hands into his coat pockets, warming them against the cold. "You go ahead and eat. I'll keep watch here until you get back."

He wondered, himself, what he was looking for. His curiosity led him to pick up a charred remnant of lumber to poke at the pile of gray ashes and blackened objects. He found a spot where the top floor had apparently collapsed. Part of the roof sat atop the heap. It was burned at the edges but only seared on the shingles.

The only thing he could figure might have happened to keep it all from burning was when the roof pitch landed on top of the first and second stories of the building, it did so with such a "thud" that it blocked air from getting in to feed the flames. The flames had starved for oxygen and a partial section of the upstairs guest rooms now were clumped before him.

What treasures lay in that pile? Would the hotel safe be in one piece and, perhaps, its contents undamaged inside? He burrowed the wooden stick into the bottom of the pile and reefed up on the charred roof using a heavy metal headboard as leverage to pry against.

Smoke wisped upward in tiny ribbons from surrounding embers.

Hope I don't start this thing up again, the Sheriff thought.

He poked deeper with the stick, trying to avoid hot spots that remained in the cooling coals.

He heard a deep thump as the stick hit something solid. He could only hope it was the safe that sat behind the counter directly below the upstairs rooms. Pushing the stick to the side, he could see the outline of a bureau. Its frame was tweaked and the mirror shattered and blackened.

He prodded lower and unearthed a saddle bag that flipped away from him. Knowing there would be leather between the two saddle bags, he slid the stick into a position to retrieve the full set.

The leather was scorched and blackened as if flames had reached it before the roof pitch saved it. He brushed the ashes from its sides. The leather thong that held the flap closed had burned off and the top lifted easily.

He pulled some gold coins and items of clothing from its depths. Not a lot of money but it was someone's grubstake he presumed. He'd have to find out if it belonged to Tyler Washington or this Everett Simmons fellow. It struck him that he had never seen Tyler Washington carry saddlebags around. It was more his style to have a large tanned leather wallet connected to a heavy gold chain that attached to a belt loop on his banker's suit and fit in his hip pocket leaving the gold chain to dangle for decoration. He had seen that often. It hung down low enough for the gold to appear flashy — too flashy for the small settlement. Or anyone looking to snatch and grab the whole lot off the banker. He'd tried to warn Washington about it before.

He removed the coins from the saddlebag and put them in his pocket. He raised the flap on the second bag. The smell of scorched cow hide wafted to his nostrils.

Inside, he found what had, not long ago, been a new rawhide jacket. Where it might have been lightly tanned suede at one time, the outer sleeves and jacket were discolored from the fire. It was rolled up tight and, when he unrolled it, strips of fringe dropped down. Protected by the larger pieces, the fringe was still in good condition.

Charlie fingered the small strips of fringe between his thumb and forefinger. He laid the jacket across his bended knee and reached inside his other pocket and retrieved the single scrap of rawhide that was found outside the bank on the day of the robbery.

He edged his fingers along each piece of fringe until he came to a place where one piece of fringe was missing. He placed the piece he had carried with him since the day of the bank robbery into the vacant spot.

Was whoever owned this coat the man that had robbed the bank? It was evidence, but not enough. Even if it came from the same coat, how could he prove it got ripped off during the bank heist?

Charlie pulled the saddlebag open and looked inside. He reached his hand to the bottom of the bag and felt a sock stuffed with something inside.

When he reached into the sock, he pulled out bank notes — bills the denomination of those stolen from the Settlers' Bank. He only hoped Tyler Washington was the careful banker he thought he was and had kept some record that would prove this was the Bank's money.

Money, really, he thought, *that belonged to the people of the surrounding area.*

If these saddlebags were owned by the man called Simmons, where was he now? And, would he come back to look for his belongings which might include incriminating evidence?

Unlike Captain Collier's murder case that grew colder day by day, this case was definitely heating up.

CHAPTER FOURTEEN

Deputy Bill returned and Sheriff Jamison gave him his instructions.

"The Swanson's Hotel safe is at the bottom of that heap. Make sure no one gets near the ruins. There may be something in there that will help them get started back on their feet. Understand?"

"Yes, Sheriff. You know I'll keep a tight watch on the property."

"Until I'm sure no one did this on purpose, it's still under investigation. I can't say that it is an arsonist's crime site, yet. But, until I tell you different, treat it as such. Nobody gets near!"

"Yes, sir."

Charlie turned on his heel and started toward the Settlers' Bank. By now, he expected Tyler Washington would be moving his big body about even if he was sore from the mornings' previous activities.

Unlike earlier this morning, the boardwalk was crowded with shoppers and people going about their errands and business appointments after a midweek holiday. He touched his fingers to his hat in greeting at several ladies. He spoke a quick "Howdy" to the men not wanting to get tied up in conversation that might delay him.

Most were not surprised at his determinably brisk stride. They knew it as one he took when there was business to attend to. The hotel fire was certainly that. People returned his acknowledgment and made room for him to get by on the boardwalk to where he was going without delay.

Charlie pushed the door open on the Settlers' Bank and looked about. The teller that had given up his coat to Mrs. Swanson was at his window tending to a local's business. He looked up and acknowledged the Sheriff as he entered. Charlie raised an eyebrow that begged the question of Tyler's location. The teller nodded toward Washington's office.

The door was open a crack and Charlie pushed it wider.

Tyler Washington sat on his settee as if dazed by the previous events and as though he was not quite recovered from the experience.

"Afternoon, Tyler," Charlie spoke.

Washington looked up slowly. He brushed at his vest as if preparing to do business with an important customer.

"Afternoon, Sheriff. As you can see, I'm not ready to greet anybody properly just yet."

Charlie slung the saddlebags he carried onto Tyler's desk. He turned the dark leather-cushioned chair to face Tyler and sat down.

"Recognize these?"

"No."

"They aren't yours?"

"No. Where'd they come from and why are you asking me? I don't have a need for saddlebags. In fact, I don't even own a horse. I rent a horse and buggy from the Swansons when I need transportation. Or, take the stage," he added.

"I was down at the remains of the hotel poking around. Found these under a pile of rubble."

"I'm surprised they survived if they were in that firestorm!"

"Found a few other things as well. But, these interested me most. Can you tell me what you might have had in your room at the hotel?"

"It doesn't take much maintenance for me, Sheriff. All I had was an extra suit, a heavy overcoat and underwear. I'm sure they burnt up in the flames. I need to get down to the tailors as soon as I rest a bit and order some new clothes."

"No bank papers? Nothing that might belong here, instead of there?"

"Not that I can think of. Just what are you implying, Sheriff?"

Charlie stretched his legs out and dug in his pants' pocket. He pulled the gold coins out and placed them on the banker's desk. Then, flipped one to Washington.

"Don't suppose there'd be anyway to identify these?"

Washington turned the coin in his fingers and studied the date.

"Not really. I can see the mint mark and the year it was pressed. That's it."

"What about paper money?"

"You don't mean bills survived in that mess, do you?"

"They were in the bottom of one pocket of the saddlebags."

"Interesting." Tyler Washington shook his head in amazement. "I'd of bet paper money, or anything that fragile, would never have survived. Why, I'd figure these coins would be a glob formed from a melted puddle."

"They were protected by a rawhide jacket stuffed on top of 'em," Charlie said and dug out a bill to hand to Tyler.

"Now, here, we might have something, Sheriff. Depending on where it was printed, there'd be a number... " Tyler brought the bill closer to his eyes and picked up his nose-pinching glasses from a table nearby.

"Do you have a list of numbers on the money that was stolen from the bank?"

"Some. Depends on the denomination. This one might be too small to bother with. Now, if you got a hundred or maybe even a twenty... "

Charlie pulled the remaining bills from his jacket pocket. He unfolded them and sorted through them.

Tyler watched with interest.

"Now, I did have one of the tellers copy some numbers down one day when we were slow. Had a few bundles of twenties. Most of those went with the robber."

The Sheriff handed him several of the bills, "I'll need a receipt for those if I need to leave them," he said.

"Of course."

Tyler raised himself slowly from the settee and motioned to a second teller sitting at a desk behind the counter.

When he reached the office door he asked, "Yes, sir, Mr. Washington?"

"Please make two records of these bills. List their numbers. Bring the records and the bills back to me when you finish."

"Yes, sir."

The teller hurried away to complete his assigned task.

"I'll get the books out today and see if any of the numbers match," Tyler told the Sheriff.

"I'll just wait and take the a copy of the list and the bills with me for evidence in case this pans out."

Charlie rose up from the chair and slid it back in place.

"Thanks for your help."

"Certainly, Sheriff. I want whoever did this caught as badly as you and my customers do."

The teller returned and handed the money and lists to Tyler and left, closing the door behind himself.

Tyler placed the bills into the sheet of paper showing their numbers and folded it into a tri-fold to secure and protect them. He pulled his desk drawer out and retrieved an envelope with the bank's return address printed in the corner. He stuffed the paper and bills inside and handed the envelope to the Sheriff.

Charlie carefully placed the bundle into his coat pocket. His intent was to lock the packet up in the heavy safe that was bolted to the floor in the back room of his office. That, along with the other evidence he had collected would be protected until he could catch the thief and take both him and the evidence to court.

Charlie hurried back to his office to secure his bundle and write up a report to put with it so he didn't forget any details when the time came to testify.

But, his major problem now was still to find whoever owned the saddlebags, arrest him and get him into jail in the first place.

Charlie puzzled over that while he sat at his desk carefully writing his report in crude letters and misspelled words.

While Sheriff Jamison searched for answers to several cases, two of which he considered might be connected, and the townspeople tried to decide how to put the pieces of their town and wellbeing back together, Clay had traveled the distance to his old home place.

He reined Buckshot in at the copse of cottonwoods near his parents' former homestead, occupied now by new residents. He watched a short time while younger children played in the yard and older ones performed their chores.

He rode on hoping to not bother the new family with its freshly built home situated in the same spot the cabin had been. Livestock now filled the old corral as he passed it riding down the familiar trail.

Flashes of his past struck Clay's mind. As clear as the day it happened he relived the loss of his parents, his rescue, and finding Captain Collier along the road that led to the Collier Ranch. Dead and stripped of his possessions.

The memories jogged him from his reverie and, mentally, he forced the past behind him.

He gently nudged Buckshot on toward his destination of the Collier Ranch.

CHAPTER FIFTEEN

Once again on Collier property, Clay soon neared the house.

He remembered his conversation with the Captain as he prepared to leave the ranch that fateful day. He also recalled the two voices he heard near the bunkhouse before the Captain left for town and failed to return.

One was a woman's high-pitched voice pinched to a whisper so low that he heard only sketchy words broken by long silences in-between.

A man's voice, gruffer but more audible than the woman's, still clung in his memory.

Who was that man? And the woman? Clay knew of no other woman within miles of the ranch. Other than Mrs. Collier, herself.

Why were they meeting so secretly? And why did the sketchy conversation give him a sense of concern?

Torn between intruding on a private conversation and feeling threatened, Clay had crept closer to the wall that held the one small window in the bunkhouse. He was alone, having gone to gather his gear before rounding up cattle on the north quarter of the Collier's property.

He didn't like having to be a brush hand. But, being a cowboy, the job sometimes called for getting off his horse and going after critters that were determined to make your life miserable.

The rest of the outfit was already headed for the Truckee River with the remainder of the cattle. The easier to gather livestock were being moved to a new pasture where the grass and sage were greening early offering better feed for the herd.

He was to meet up with two other riders near the large cottonwood tree at the edge of the outer grazing land. *No time to waste*, he thought, but took his concern about the ongoing conversation seriously.

"I got no problem doin' it," the man's words reached Clay's ears.

"Be sure ... can tie this ... to me," the woman's comment was hard to make out.

Tie what to whom? Clay wondered. But, then, the conversation broke off and he heard the Captain call to his wife. His booming echo sounded from the ranch house. Clay wondered why he would be calling so loudly. Wasn't Mrs. Collier somewhere inside? Perhaps she had visited the outhouse? He felt a twinge of suspicion. Surely, it wasn't Mrs. Collier he heard talking to what seemed to be a stranger to him by being an unrecognizable voice to his ears.

Finally, when he decided the bunkhouse was empty, Clay retrieved his bedroll and went to tie it behind his saddle on his horse, Adonis, at the front yard hitching post. He saw Mrs. Collier approach the house and start up the steps.

"There you are!" the Captain said, his words louder and clearer than those that still puzzled Clay.

"Yes. I was checking out a new garden spot. Did you need something?"

"I'll be leaving now. I've asked Clay to check on you now and then. I'm sure you'll be safe while I'm gone," the Captain's words, though lower, still reached him clearly.

"Fine," Mrs. Collier said from the yard. Clay saw her glance his way, then turn back to the Captain.

"I thought he was out on the range."

"I'm sending him to the north pasture to meet up with Kit and Cookie. Once he has those strays in hand, they can meet up with the rest. I'm sure he'll be back before dark. The rest of the men will take the cattle on to the new pasture. If you're uncomfortable being here alone, I'll give Clay a job that keeps him close to the house." The Captain had come down the porch stairs and now stood on the ground facing his wife.

Mrs. Collier raised her apron to wipe her hands.

"Do as you wish," she answered, being one to never ask for special favors. "I'll get you some food to take with you for the road," she returned over her shoulder as she moved up the steps to the porch.

"Better hurry. I'm getting a late start as it is."

The front door closed behind Mrs. Collier while the Captain went to double check his horse's cinch while waiting for his grub sack.

Clay untied Adonis, still wondering about the secret conversation he'd been privy to earlier. *Could the woman have been Mrs. Collier?* He pulled his horse away from the hitching rail and led it slowly up to where the Captain stood re-buckling the cinch.

"Always got to remember to stick a knee in this old fella's gut," the Captain told him by way of greeting. "He's a good one to hold his breath when you put the saddle on. He's getting on in age but he learned that trick early. Never was able to break him of it."

"Have a good trip," Clay said as he prepared to mount.

133

"There's been a change of plans. I want you to stay close by the house and see that Maggie doesn't have any trouble."

Clay felt a sense of relief that he wouldn't be yanking calves out of the brush where the mommas had dropped them or fighting with the cows to drag their babies away. What stock remained behind was sure to be cows with newborn calves. *They could stay together a few more days and be pretty content with that,* he thought. And, he'd be happy to do something else in the meantime.

"Kit and Cookie are about to leave with the grub wagon to catch up to the other boys. They'll be able to get there a lot faster now that they don't have to wait for you. I'll tell them to let the crew know you won't be joining them on the trail."

"Thanks, Captain," Clay said without further comment about the situation.

"I'm depending on you to watch out for the place and Maggie. I know I can trust you to do that."

"Yes, Sir, Captain," Clay confirmed he would carry out the Captain's intentions.

"I should be back before night fall tomorrow."

"Yes, Sir," Clay said.

The Captain secured his rifle in its hand-stamped scabbard attached to the saddle along with the other hardware already affixed there. The gun was mostly for snakes. He didn't like riding around with pistols strapped to his sides. He relied on the rifle for anything that might arise.

Clay observed the rifle, knowing that it would be no good in close combat, if the Captain was ever confronted by anyone that surprised him.

Clay raised his hand as they parted and the Captain rode toward the chuck wagon. He hesitated for only a moment. Clay saw Cookie glance his way and nod his head to indicate he understood the Captain.

The Captain walked his horse away a distance past the gate before urging it into a gallop down the road toward town.

That was the last Clay saw of his mentor — alive.

CHAPTER SIXTEEN

Instead of mounting into the saddle, Clay led Adonis back toward the corral. His intent was to remove the saddle and the rest of the tack and turn the horse loose in a pen next to calves still needing inspection.

He passed the rear of the chuck wagon as Cookie moved himself into a more comfortable position for the long ride out to a temporary camp. He clutched the reins of the team tight in his big hands.

"You, Sally. Enjoy your night in the bunkhouse," Cookie taunted him.

Kit sat his own horse to ride behind the wagon. He looked from the older man to the younger one with curiosity to see what the reaction would be.

"Guess you'll miss my fine cookin' tonight."

"Just following the boss's orders," Clay said. He wanted to tell him to enjoy his night on the hard ground next to a diminishing campfire. "Been looking at those black clouds coming in. Hope you don't wake up soaked in the morning while I'm enjoying the warmth of the stove in the bunkhouse and Mrs. Collier's biscuits and gravy for breakfast," Clay retorted.

"You're going to miss out on my camp beans. Got some fine brown sugar and ham to add to 'em," Cookie chided him good-naturedly.

Cookie was considerably older than Clay and he had been working on the ranch much longer. *Could he be the man's voice he heard earlier in the day? No,* Clay thought. As far as he knew, Cookie and Kit were the only hands around the ranch at the time. The rest of the crew had already left to move the herd several hours before.

Kit was much younger but didn't seem the type to be cavorting with some woman. He was usually quiet and kept to himself in the bunkhouse.

Who could the male voice belong to? Clay tried to shake the memory of the broken conversation from his mind. It probably meant nothing.

Now, Clay tried to ignore Cookie's taunts and moved to Adonis' side away from the chuck wagon to concentrate on unbuckling the cinch and removing the saddle. With the horse between himself and Cookie he hoped the man would go on about his business and leave him be.

He heard the slap of the reins against horsehide as Cookie sent the chuck wagon rolling out of the yard. Clay watched as they took to a rutted section of trail that went in the direction the herd of cows would travel. It would take the wagon a bit to reach the predetermined site designated as the place to set up camp, have the evening meal and bed down for the night.

Clay opened the gate and let Adonis into the corral. By then, Cookie was already off the dusty trail and onto low-grazed pasture in the distance. Clay could barely see the rear of the wagon as he scooped a couple of handfuls of oats into a feeder for Adonis before tending to the calves.

The sun was setting when he considered his day's work

done. He dusted himself off and was washing up in a small granite basin on a wooden crate sitting vertical on the porch next to the bunkhouse door. He prepared to go to the house to check in on Mrs. Collier. Before he finished drying off, Mrs. Collier opened the back door and rang the triangle to call him to supper.

It had been a peaceful day without any disturbance once the chuck wagon left. Only a few ornery calves had refused to cooperate with Clay as he inspected and treated them for their usual cuts and occasional runny nose or weepy eyes.

For a few seconds, as he walked toward the house, Clay felt left out from the trail drive and he wished he had gone with the other men. He would miss Cookie's meals. Since he moved into the bunkhouse his palate had become accustomed to the beans and biscuits Cookie supplied. He had learned to eat with appreciation and not question the contents of the cook pot.

Still it had been awhile since he'd had a civilized dinner in the ranch house, as well.

Clay raised his hand in a wave to let Maggie know he had heard the call to eat.

"Are you ready for dinner?" Mrs. Collier asked him when he reached the back porch.

"Yes, Ma'am. Captain said I should stay close and finish working the calves. But I've done the most of it."

"You must come in and eat something. I've watched you working hard all day. I kept a plate of food warm for you so I wouldn't interrupt your work."

"Thank you. I've washed up already and I sure am hungry. I appreciate it."

When Clay moved the chair out to sit down, Mrs. Collier placed a heavy plate filled with potatoes, gravy and a large chunk of beef roast in front of him. She sat a relish dish with pickles next to his plate.

She poured a strong cup of coffee for him and sat a cup of tea down at her place across the table from him.

"Aren't you going to eat, too?" Clay queried when he saw she failed to dish up food for herself.

"With the Captain in town, I ate early so I could get busy with one of the chores that usually gets neglected. Besides, you really mustn't worry about me. There was nothing eventful around here, today, unless you consider the rooster attacking the goose a danger. The goose won, by the way."

Clay chewed the beef savoring its rich flavor imparted by excellent pasture and corn fattening while he listened to her story.

He swallowed quickly in order to chuckle at the story. "That's not a surprise. The goose thinks he can take on anything. The rooster should have known better." *Why was she telling him this insignificant tale?* Clay wondered. *Had her day really been that boring?*

Mrs. Collier moved to top off his cup of coffee for him and freshened tea for herself. She brought the cups back to the table and sat them down. She brushed at imaginary crumbs, or wrinkles, he couldn't tell which, from the tablecloth before she moved her chair aside to sit down and join him while she added sugar to the liquid in her cup and stirred it slowly before enjoying her drink.

Clay finished his meal and slid his chair back to relax with his coffee mug.

"How bad off was the rooster?" Clay continued her previous conversation for lack of anything better to talk about. "Do we still have an alarm clock?"

"He took himself off to the chicken coop and ate up the pity from the hens. I think he'll still be crowing in the mornings."

"Well, then, your day wasn't without excitement," Clay

said with amusement in his voice.

"Fortunately, there was nothing more serious," Mrs. Collier said.

"I'll be finishing up with those calves tomorrow so, if you need anything, just give a shout," Clay assured her.

"Thank you. I'll be busy with my chores. I can't imagine any reason to need help. But I shall call out, if I do."

"Good. Thank you, Ma'am, for dinner. I always have enjoyed your cookin'."

"You've certainly grown up, Clay. I so remember your younger days tagging along with Captain and the other cowboys around the ranch. Now, here you are a grown man, ready to protect me from any sudden danger. My, when the Captain and I didn't have any children, I didn't know who I could trust up until now."

Clay took his hat from the peg by the door and said "goodnight."

"Goodnight, Clay."

Clay awoke in the middle of the night. *Was that the sound of horse's hooves diminishing into the distance?* He strained to figure it out, listening closely but hearing nothing now that he was fully awake.

He rose from his bunk and edged the door to the bunkhouse open a sliver. Studying the ranch house he saw the light in the Captain and his wife's bedroom suddenly extinguish.

CHAPTER SEVENTEEN

Now, these years later as Clay squatted beneath the open window of the ranch house, he heard Mrs. Collier and the man loud and clear. There was no doubt in his mind they were arguing.

"You're sitting pretty, now, aren't you?" the man's voice boomed. "Well, you can thank me for that! And that's probably all I'll get!"

"All you'll get? I tried to get in touch with you to get my share of the money and couldn't find you," Mrs. Collier raised her voice to a near shout.

"Well, what's fair's fair. When I was a kid you left me hanging high and dry. Guess I musta learned it from you," the man replied.

"You know I couldn't take you with me. The Captain didn't know I'd been married before. He sure didn't know I had a child. I wasn't about to mess up a good thing when I could leave you where you'd be safe."

"I begged for you to come back. Watched the door every night wondering where you were and why you'd left me behind. The woman you left me with was too old to take care of a kid. I ended up taking care of her and nearly starving to death until she died and I got out of there."

Clay heard footsteps as if someone was pacing the floor.

"If I hadn't looked you up, I'd have never known where you had gone. Not that it matters now. Look, you promised if I took care of your husband you'd see to it I got a piece of this ranch. You said you'd make me a foreman. You said we'd enlarge the ranch by buying up nearby properties after I ran the current owners off for you."

"You never returned with the money the Captain was carrying that night. How was I supposed to do all that if there wasn't any cash to do it with? I ought to turn you in for killing the Captain!"

"You do and you'll hang right along with me. I don't know if Nevada has ever hung a woman but they might be willing to start. It was all your idea and you know it."

"You can't prove a thing!" Mrs. Collier shouted back.

"Well, neither can you!"

"You better get out of here before the boys return to the bunkhouse. They find you here like this, they'll sure have your hide."

"Is that any way to treat your only son?"

"Is that any way to treat your own mother?"

"Look, I had to put the money somewhere safe until things cooled down a bit. Ended up having to rob a bank just to survive until I felt we could chance spending what your husband was carrying on him."

Mrs. Collier's voice quieted.

Clay had to strain to hear her words.

She pleaded with the man, "Look, we can still do this. You bring that money — maybe it's safe to use it now — and I'll still make you the foreman. Jesse is getting old and shouldn't be doing that job any more anyway."

"And how do I trust you any more now than before?"

"You've got my word. I promise we'll build this place up to be the biggest cattle ranch in Nevada. I just need your help. Bring me the money and you'll see. We can put all this behind us and still be the biggest ranchers in the area."

Clay heard the front door slam and heavy boots stomp down the porch steps. Lighter footsteps crossed the floor toward the window he hid beneath. He secluded himself in the ornamental bushes close to the building until he could make a break for it without being seen.

So, it was all a plan of Mrs. Colliers'! She had set her husband's fate in motion and then tried to double cross a son from a previous marriage. Clay put the pieces together in his mind.

He heard the horse ride across the hard-packed dirt of the front yard and then pick up speed as it went down the path to the road that ran east and west. He wondered which direction the rider would go.

Either direction he rode, Clay didn't plan on letting him reach his destination alone.

Not if he had anything to do with it! At least, not under his own power. Clay hurried to the trees to untie Buckshot and head back through the pasture to where it connected with the main road.

CHAPTER EIGHTEEN

Clay watched to see which direction the rider turned when he left the Collier property.

West.

Once he determined that the man was, indeed, headed in that direction he moved to follow.

He was well aware that he had no weapons to defend himself, yet he returned to the site beside the mound of dirt where he had hidden from the rider on the trip to the ranch. He climbed up the backside of the dirt and positioned himself carefully.

There had been no doubt in his mind that the man would have to pass this way, reversing the incoming trip. He soon heard the loping sound of hoof beats coming down the road. As the resonance drew closer he crouched, ready to spring. Surprise was his only defense. He had to get the upper hand on the man before he knew what hit him.

As the horse came alongside where the path narrowed forcing the rider tight to the base of Clay's hiding place, Clay lunged and knocked the rider off his horse and onto the ground with a sudden "whump!"

He heard a loud grunt as he knocked the wind out of his enemy. The horse whinnied and raced off down the road toward town.

"What the hell?" The man uttered.

Clay straddled the prone man's back and worked to relieve him of his guns.

The stunned and winded man struggled and fought to roll over.

"No, you don't," Clay told him as he tossed one pistol after the other away with his left hand while he shoved the man's head down and his face into the dirt with his right.

"You're going back to town all right. But you're going with me and direct to the Sheriff. I'm sure he'll be real interested in hearing what you and Mrs. Collier cooked up. You're going to clear my name and take the punishment you deserve for killing the Captain! I'm sure Mr. Washington will be glad to know who robbed his bank, too."

"You don't know what you're talking about!" The man spit blood and dirt from his mouth when he managed to turn his head sideways.

"I heard you and Mrs. Collier arguing. I know you killed the Captain and then robbed the bank. Heck, I'd bet you were the one that set fire to the hotel, too! I'm taking you in to confess."

Clay moved to the side of the man and crouched there while he got his breath. Then he tugged him by one arm. "Get up! You're coming with me."

The dilemma now became how to keep his prisoner under control and both of them ride double on his horse.

He whistled for Buckshot to come to him. The horse was not as quick to respond as Adonis had been. Clay needed to make the shrill sound again in order to draw Buckshot away from grazing the few old blades of grass.

The man still staggered as he tried to recover from

Clay's surprise attack that had overwhelmed him.

At last, Buckshot nickered and stopped alongside Clay. Clay reached up and removed a short lasso from a leather loop on the saddle. He shook the rope out with one hand while gripping the man's two hands behind his back. Quickly he wrapped the bindings around the man's one wrist. The man struggled to put up a fight. Clay jerked the strap around and clutched the free arm the man swung toward him. Pinching his wrists tight, he pressed both hands together in front of the man and reefed the bindings tight.

The man swung his head down in an attempt to connect a blow to Clay's face. Clay dodged the assault and pulled the rope until it cut into the man's wrists.

Clay, sweating from the struggle, faced the man with more strength than he thought he could muster.

"That ought to hold you. You want to keep those hands, just try something else. Now, either you can walk all the way back to the Sheriff or, if you get lucky, we'll find your horse up ahead. Chances are he'll be clear back to the stable eating hay before long though."

It was going to be a slow, miserable trip back to town if Clay didn't come up with a better mode of transportation for his prisoner.

The only option was to boost the man into the saddle and position himself behind him.

Riding double would still be slow but wouldn't take as long as walking the man all the way.

He didn't much care for handling the reins by reaching around both sides of the man. But, he knew it would be more dangerous for his own safety if he kept his prisoner behind him where Clay couldn't see what he was up to.

Finally, he chose the alternative to the man's walking and cautiously put him on the horse.

Even though Clay stayed on the main road, the ride was

slowed by Buckshot's struggle to carry the extra weight. He tired quickly and Clay was forced to stop to rest the horse. At times, he dismounted and walked short distances to make the trip easier on Buckshot.

Clay remounted and was barely back behind the saddle, but not settled properly, when the man kicked his heels into Buckshot's sides. The action caused Buckshot to lunge forward quickly and break into a struggling run.

"Whoa!" Clay shouted as he tried to calm the startled horse before it injured itself or tossed both of them to the ground.

"I ought to strangle you right here for pulling that trick!" Clay said in exasperation.

"What good would that do you?"

As much as Clay hated to admit it, he was right. If he killed him, now, there'd be no way to get a confession out of him. There'd be no proof he was the killer instead of himself. He was sure the Sheriff would believe Mrs. Collier over him. He didn't know how he was going to do it but he had to make her son tell the truth and sign a piece of paper admitting to their crimes.

"Pull something like that again and I will wring your neck. I've still got two free hands and some strong leather reins even if I don't have a gun. You've caused me enough problems, I'd be justified. Not including the fact that you killed a very good friend of mine." In his mind, he could not understand what would make the Captain's wife set out to have her husband killed. *Greed*, he guessed. *You just couldn't trust some people, even if you thought you knew them well,* he figured.

In this case, it would have been good if the Captain had known the woman better before he married her.

"I told you I'd seen you somewhere before. It was at the ranch, wasn't it? Maybe you didn't see me, but I saw you. As

I was leaving I saw you talking to Captain Collier. Wish I'd a figured that out while we were still in town. You could have burnt up in the fire along with everything else, if I'd known then."

"So, it was you that set the fire!" He wished someone other than himself had heard the man admit it.

"Prove it! Nobody will believe it," the man tried to remove the suspicion from himself.

"I wasn't there the morning of the fire. You'd have had a tough time pulling that off," Clay replied.

"I'd a figured something out and dumped you in there, if I'd remembered where I saw you before."

"I bet you would have, if you could."

CHAPTER NINETEEN

When Clay reached the outskirts of town with his prisoner, the first thing that came into view was the O'Flannery mansion. It was still daylight and the waning sunlight allowed Bradley and Amy to play outside in the large yard surrounding the house.

He didn't know which he hated worse, having to haul this killer double or having the children see him come into town with his prisoner.

Bradley will probably make a big to do about it. He could already hear his young voice calling toward the house, "Holly! Holly! Holly!"

Amy had one mitten-covered hand wrapped around an upright rail of the wrought-iron fence. She poked her face into the gap between two bars and stared at him as if frozen there.

He didn't even dare to raise his hand and wave in acknowledgement. He hadn't ridden this far in this manner to chance losing his only proof of innocence let alone make it known that he knew the children. He couldn't trust that, should his prisoner escape, he might not go after them for revenge against his captor.

Gradually, Clay began to see a rider here and there and a few people on the boardwalk hurrying to finish their business before the stores closed for the evening and they rushed home to dinner.

The closer they rode to the Sheriff's Office, the heavier the traffic became. A stagecoach rushed into town, its passengers anticipating a meal and a good nights rest at the hotel.

What a surprise they'll have when they get there and the hotel is in ruins, Clay thought.

But, that wasn't his problem.

He was on his way to a building much closer than that. And, with each step Buckshot took, he felt more anxious. If his captive was going to make a break for it, he'd have to try to do it soon. Clay kept his body tense, ready to spring after him if necessary.

He heard people chattering as he moved past them. Their curiosity at two strangers riding in on one horse, like they were, caused a stir amidst them. They silenced and stared after Clay and the man.

"Hey Mister, what happened? Did you catch a bandit?" A young boy called out to him.

Clay ignored his question.

If it weren't for Holly, he thought, *that well could be Bradley.* He feared that Bradley might try to convince Holly to let him take her and Amy in tow and come to view the excitement.

He hoped Holly could restrain Bradley — and herself.

Regardless of what concern Holly might have, this situation wouldn't be over until they reached the Sheriff's Office and the man sat in a jail cell awaiting trial. He didn't want to risk the possibility that things could go badly if the man decided to make a break for it. Someone could get hurt. He didn't want it to be Holly or one of the kids.

When they reached the hitching rail in front of the Sheriff's Office, Sheriff Jamison was coming out his door shoving his hat on his head. He straightened up and looked Clay straight in the eyes.

"What you got there?" he asked before Clay dismounted.

"Someone to warm your jail. He's good at that! I'll explain as soon as we get him inside."

On the ground, Clay looked back up at the man and warned, "Don't get any ideas. While I don't have a gun, the Sheriff does and probably plenty of other people around here do, too."

He dropped the horse's reins over the rail and wrapped them twice. Then, returned to the saddle where he ordered the man to get down.

"Untie me so I can. My hands are numb now. I can't feel anything with them to do anybody any harm."

"No, I will not! You hitch your hands around the saddle horn and throw your leg over. On this side! Don't try anything stupid like dismounting on the other side and getting the horse to shy."

The man shrugged. He gripped the saddle horn as he was instructed and struggled, whether for show or through necessity, to lift his leg in front of him and across the saddle above the horn before moving his hands. He slid his back down the horse's body and stood facing Clay with his hands still tied in front.

Clay clutched his arm and tugged him toward the Sheriff.

Curious, the Sheriff opened his office door. As he turned to go in behind the two men he looked back at the small crowd that had gathered.

"You good folks go on back to your homes. The show's

well over now."

Mumbling to themselves and each other, the people moved away.

The stagecoach driver, who had left his passengers milling around in front of the burned out hotel, reached the Office before the Sheriff shut the door.

"Sheriff! What are we supposed to do about grub and beds for the night?"

"Well, we got a boarding house and a saloon or two that serves food. I'm sure, if nothing else, the travelers can eat. If you can't find accommodations, you might have to drive 'em on to the next settlement. Don't think you want to try to make Reno tonight, though. That's another full day's travel."

The driver scratched his head. "Well, I guess if that's the best we can do. We have a contract with Swanson, though. He ain't going to like losing the business I'm sure."

"I don't think he's going to like finding out the news that he lost the building when he gets back in town either. Guess it's up to you to solve your own problem. I've got things to take care of inside."

The driver turned back toward the stagecoach as the Sheriff closed the door and sized up the two men standing in the middle of the room.

"And who might you two be?"

"This is Captain Collier's real killer. Not me!" Clay said.

"You do look a bit familiar," Sheriff Jamison said.

"I should. I was the boy the Captain took in when my folks were killed."

"And him?" The Sheriff pointed to the other man.

"Near as I can tell, he's Mrs. Collier's son."

"The Captain and his Mrs. never had any kids, near as I know."

"Not the Captain, Sheriff. Mrs. Collier had another life

before the Captain met her. He's the result of that. Everett Simmons near as I understand."

Upon hearing the name, the Sheriff raised his eyebrows.

All the while the second man remained silent, clenching words behind his teeth and taut lips.

Clay shoved him toward the Sheriff's desk.

Charlie removed his hat slowly and placed it on a peg in the wall behind his desk where it was convenient to retrieve at a moment's notice.

He sat down in his wooden office chair.

The man slumped into another straight-backed chair in front of the desk and placed his tied hands on top where an oil lamp sat ready to be lit at the first sign of darkness.

"What's your story?" Charlie asked.

"Take these ties off me," the man demanded. "The damn things are cutting through my skin."

"Not a chance," Clay answered for the Sheriff.

The man slumped back against the slats of the wooden chair back. He moved his hands to his lap and stared straight ahead.

"Sheriff, the night that mob dragged me through town, I was out looking for the Captain like his wife asked me to. I'd found him laying alongside the road between here and the ranch. He was already dead when I got there. His horse and all his belongings were gone. He was darned near picked clean ant it wasn't no real buzzard that did it. I loaded him onto my horse and brought him in," Clay explained.

"Earlier the day before, right before the Captain left, I overheard his Mrs. and someone whispering. I couldn't see who it was but I knew the only woman around was Mrs. Collier. Then she lied to the Captain when he asked her where she'd been."

"I didn't think much about it then. Who'd of thought his own wife would set him up to be killed?"

"Are you trying to tell me Mrs. Collier was in on this," the Sheriff stumbled for a name, "Bingham, isn't it? Now, I recollect who you are!"

"Yes. Clay Bingham. And, yes, Mrs. Collier plotted his death with her son here. I heard it confirmed when I rode out to the ranch to see if Mrs. Collier could help me clear myself. I couldn't believe it, either!"

"Anyway, I heard a horse coming and got off to the side of the road. When I recognized this fellow who'd acted suspiciously like he was following me, I hid until he got by, then took a back trail to the ranch."

The man kicked his toe at the bottom of the desk.

The Sheriff stared at him and he dropped his foot to the floor.

"I saw his horse out by the bunkhouse and, when I crept up alongside the main house I could hear the two of them arguing. Seems he never brought all the cash the Captain was carrying back to Mrs. Collier like he was supposed to."

"That true?" The Sheriff asked the sullen man.

He got no reaction.

"That right? Your name's Everett Simmons?"

The man ignored him.

"Anyway, he had stayed at the hotel the couple of nights I did. I saw him at the Barbershop. After that, I never saw him again until he rode up behind me on the trail."

"The hotel, you say?" The Sheriff asked.

"Yes."

"You know the hotel burned."

"I heard that, Actually, saw the flames from the O'Flannery house way early this morning."

"O'Flannery's?"

Clay didn't want to explain why he was staying there. Right now, he didn't think he had to. He wasn't under arrest. And, so far, neither was his captive.

The light was getting dimmer in the room. The Sheriff stood up.

"You two wait right here," he said and moved down the hall.

Soon he was back. He slapped the saddlebags he had retrieved from the hotel debris onto his desktop.

"I understand there were only two people staying in the hotel the night before the fire. Tyler Washington was one of them."

The man looked at the saddlebags in surprise.

"Now, what's interesting is, Washington pretty much proved these weren't his. Recognize 'em? You?" The Sheriff looked at the bound man.

The man shook his head weakly.

"Look a little closer. What's the matter, too dark in here to see?" The Sheriff struck a match and lit the lamp on his desk. Then he began pulling items out of the bags. He started with the right side which, with the gold coins removed, only had a couple of socks and a shirt in it.

Then, he stuffed his hand into the left bag and pulled out the rawhide jacket edged in fringe.

Immediately Clay recognized the jacket with the rawhide strips around the bottom and down the arms.

"That's his Sheriff. He wore that when I first saw him at the hotel. Then, again, when he was following me around town."

"What you got to say for yourself, Everett Simmons? If that's your real name — " the Sheriff broke off and waited for an answer.

"Never seen that stuff before in my life. You can't prove it's mine, even if you try."

"Guess what else I found in there," the Sheriff pulled the gold coins out of his pocket and dropped them onto his desk letting them clink together in the middle of the wood.

Simmons stared straight ahead without letting his eyes follow the sound of the weight hitting the desktop.

When he got no reaction, Charlie withdrew the stack of bills wrapped inside the paper. "These were in there, too. Under the coat. Now, I figure, if this coat is yours — and, if this piece of fringe I got here that I found outside the bank when it was robbed fits into an empty space on it, which it does — that all means whoever owns this coat robbed the bank the other day."

"Again. You got no proof." Simmons swung his legs to the side as if to get up from in front of the desk.

"The jacket is his. Tyler Washington can vouch for that. We saw him wearing it at the hotel at breakfast. And, he wore it in the Barbershop. Ask the Barber. He can testify to that, too."

Clay shoved Everett back down.

"I've tried to figure out how he happened to lose a scrap of it. I found this tag-end lying on the boardwalk outside the bank. Only thing I can figure is he must have caught the trim on the hitching rail that's right in front of the bank when he was coming to rob it. Must of felt the tug and decided to go back to his horse and take the jacket off. Maybe that jolted him into thinking it would be too noticeable and leave more people able to identify him if he wore it in the robbery. Undo his hands, Bingham."

"What?" Clay wanted to ask the Sheriff if he was loco, but thought better of it.

As Clay began to undo Simmons' hands, the man lunged across the desk and knocked the lamp onto the evidence lying on top.

Clay tackled Simmons before he could reach Charlie but flames shot up where lamp oil spilled and the flame on the wick ignited the oil.

As quick as Simmons was, the Sheriff was quicker. He

dashed the lamp away from the items on his desk and onto the floor. Only the globe settled on top of the rawhide jacket.

The first fumes of the oil on the floor flared but the pool of oil drowned the oxygen away and put the initial blaze out.

Charlie grabbed his long coat from the peg next to his hat and smothered what fire had caught the edge of the bills and their list of numbers.

"That wasn't a smart move, Simmons. Just proves to me you are the one that owns this coat. You're also the one that robbed the bank. I believe that, but in order to convince a judge I need one more thing."

The Sheriff felt his way around the desk and over to a wall lamp. They heard a screech as he pulled the chimney from its base and the glass was released from its prongs. Then light flooded the room as the Sheriff settled the chimney back over the lit wick.

"Go ahead, Bingham, finish untying him like I said."

Clay shook his head. He didn't think it was a good idea. But, if the Sheriff had a better one than he did, he'd have to comply.

Clay released the rope from the prisoner's wrists.

The Sheriff grasped the jacket and shoved it toward Everett.

"Put it on, Simmons," the Sheriff said as he held the coat in front of him.

Clay could smell lamp oil when the Sheriff handed it past him toward the other man.

Simmons refused.

"Put it on or I'll put it on you,' the Sheriff's voice boomed. The Sheriff began to fidget with a match stick, flipping it between his thumb and finger tips. All he had to do was strike it across his thick thumbnail and it would burst into flame. They all knew that.

For Clay and the Sheriff it was no threat. But, for Simmons who now had the coat in his hands and laying across his arms, it presented a dilemma. Saturated with lamp oil beading on the rawhide, he could go up in flames if it was set afire. Everett wasn't sure either man standing there would put the flames out.

Slowly, Simmons unfolded the coat and slid one arm in a sleeve. When the other arm was in the other sleeve he shrugged the coat up onto his shoulders. He tugged the center opening down with both hands as if admiring the workmanship of the jacket.

Clay looked at Charlie. The Sheriff wasn't so "loco" after all. He'd had a plan all along. He just wasn't sharing it, Clay realized.

Charlie reached for his ring of keys.

"Take it off!"

Simmons looked at him as if to protest but soon complied. He handed the coat back to the Sheriff.

Charlie grasped him by the arm and shoved him toward a cell.

"Don't you go nowhere, Bingham. I'm not done with you, yet. Maybe he killed Collier and maybe he didn't. I won't have a feel for that until I talk to Mrs. Collier.

Clay crossed the possibilities in his mind.

What if he talked to Mrs. Collier and she convinced him she had nothing to do with it?

That would be bad enough. Maybe she would pin it all on Simmons, he thought.

At the very least, Simmons would be in jail for bank robbery.

But, what if they both denied the killing? What would happen then? Was he any better off than he was before? He wondered. *Could the two of them possibly lay the blame on him after all?*

The Sheriff returned with the keys still clanging from the ring in his hand. He took the evidence from the desk and secured it in the safe.

"Thanks for bringing him in. You caught a bank robber and there's a reward for that. Most likely he's also an arsonist. However, until I'm convinced he's the guilty one here, in the Collier situation, I'm going to have to lock you up, too."

Clay felt his heart sink into his stomach. This wasn't turning out the way he had hoped.

CHAPTER TWENTY

Bradley's excitement at seeing Clay bring the man into town led him to rush inside the house and find Holly where she studied in her room.

"Holly! Holly!" Bradley called as he ran up the stairs sloughing snow off his boots each step of the way.

Holly's studies were already distracted by the anticipation of Clay's return. *Why wasn't he back, yet?* She reminded herself that she had spent too many days in the past worrying about a man she wasn't even sure would ever return.

"Bradley, what is it?"

"Clay — Mr. Bingham. We saw him riding with another man on his horse with him. He rode on past into town."

Clay, Clay was back! Holly thought then caught herself.

"Why would he do that, Holly?"

"I'm sure I don't know. Where is Amy?" She asked, suddenly startled that the little girl wasn't with her brother.

"She was watching them go by!"

Holly set her book aside.

"You really shouldn't leave Amy outside by herself,"

Holly scolded. After Amy's close call at the pond she was hypersensitive and overprotective where the child was concerned.

She rushed down the stairs with Bradley at her heels.

"Where do you think he was going, Holly? Do you think he was going somewhere else to stay instead of staying with us?" Bradley asked with concern. Having another male in the house piqued his interest. Especially one that was sober and wasn't afraid to take action.

"I'm sure I don't know, Bradley. Although the hotel was completely destroyed in the fire this morning, I'm told, so I hardly doubt he was headed there." Her words were tempered with trepidation and the way she answered made him look at her with shock registering on his face.

Holly sprinted across the front room and through the entry without grabbing a wrap. She was out the door and calling Amy's name into the cold air.

Darkness was falling and she didn't see the child anywhere in the yard.

"Where was she, Bradley?"

"She was staring through the gate when I left her."

"Amy!" Holly shrieked into the dark.

"Bradley, run around the house. Go to the stable, if you must. We have to find her!" Holly was near panic and thought of the many things that could have happened to Amy.

Bradley did as he was told. He ran across the footprints he and his sister had made earlier in the day near where they were trying to fashion a snowman from dwindling snow.

Amy was nowhere in sight.

Bradley ran faster, dashing to the barn and calling for Joshua.

"Amy's gone," he told the man. "We can't find her. " He

was near tears as Joshua rushed from the barn to the stable with the boy fast behind him.

They searched the stalls and found Honora hurrying down the center isle between the horse stalls. She carried a basket with vegetables from the root cellar.

"What is it?" She asked as the two rushed toward her.

"Amy," Joshua said. "Amy's missing."

"Oh my!" Honor gasped.

"She was watching Mr. Bingham ride by. She wasn't there when Holly and I got back to the gate."

Honora rushed toward the house while Bradley and Joshua finished checking the stalls.

Amy was not there among the livestock.

Holly, all but having given up, was returning to the house to get her cape and boots to go for the Sheriff.

Out of breath, Honora joined her at the door.

"Miss Holly this is terrible! Where could she be?"

"I'm going for the Sheriff. She can't be left out in the cold. It's dark outside now. What will she do? Where did she go?"

Holly was near tears as the reality gripped her senses tighter.

"Oh, Miss Holly, I am so afraid for our little girl!"

Holly ran to the closet for her wraps while Honora set the basket of vegetables on the table to wring her hands in worry.

She lit the kitchen lamp and spoke over her shoulder, "I'll put the tea pot on so you can warm up when you return. Why don't you send Joshua instead of going yourself?" Honora asked as she turned to stoke the fire and put more wood in the range.

Joshua and Bradley came through the back door.

"Did you find her?" Holly asked them anxiously.

"No," Bradley said, sobbing now.

"Oh my!" Honora gasped loudly.

"Honora! What is it?" Holly hurried back to the kitchen.

Honora covered her mouth in surprise and pointed to the kitchen floor.

There on a rug by the kitchen counter was Amy.

The cookie jar sat beside her tipped on its side with the few remaining cookies spilling out. Amy slept soundly curled on the rug with her coat still bundled around her and her knit hat, its flaps covering her ears, tied beneath her chin.

Holly quickly squatted beside her. She touched the child's cheek to reassure herself Amy was truly there.

Joshua picked the child up and cradled her in his strong arms. He followed Holly to Amy's bedroom where he laid the still sleeping girl on the coverlet.

"Thank you, Joshua. Please tell Bradley to stay inside now and get ready for the evening meal. This little one already ate hers. She probably won't awake until morning." Holly prepared to pull Amy's outerwear off and slip her beneath the covers.

When she returned to the kitchen, Honora, having regained her composure, was busily preparing dinner.

"The teapot is full and the tea is ready for you," she told Holly. Then she asked,

"Shall I set a plate for Mr. Clay, Miss Holly?" Honora asked as she sat the stacked plates and silverware on the table.

"I don't know, Honora. He may be too busy to get here when we eat. You may need to keep a plate of food warm for him for later."

"Very well. I'll put a setting on the table for him anyway. If he doesn't arrive in time, I'll set things to keep warm, just in case he gets here later."

"Thank you, Honora," Holly said as, now that Amy was safe, concern for Clay wormed its way into her mind.

163

At dinner time Clay still had not shown up.

Holly called for Bradley to wash up for supper.

The two of them sat down to their meal. They ate in relative silence, except for when Bradley periodically broke the quiet to attempt to tell her what he saw.

He hoped to avert the possibility that Holly might punish him for Amy's disappearance. He talked quickly and breathlessly.

"He had some man riding in front of him," Bradley said for the umpteenth time.

"Bradley, I told you, we'll find out what happened when Clay gets here. Now, eat your dinner."

Amy stumbled sleepily into the dining room, tugging her favorite blanket behind her. She looked at Holly with her eyes barely open as she rubbed them with the one empty fist.

"Amy! I thought you'd sleep through the night. What are you doing up?"

Amy ignored her question.

"I saw it, too. I was cold and coming to the house when Bradley started running up the stairs and hollering for you. Nobody was around to help me get a cookie. "

"Yes, I know you were there at the gate," Holly replied.

"Mr. Bingham looked right at me while the other man watched the people on the street."

"He looked — upset — or something," Bradley added.

"Determined, perhaps," Holly let the children rope her into their conversation.

"Like this," Bradley said and worked his face into a copy of Clay's expression.

"Enough! Can't we have at least one meal in peace before I have to go back to school?"

Immediately Holly wanted to bite her tongue. She hadn't planned to mention returning to school and ruin the time she was home by worrying the children. Their story bothered her and, after the terror of Amy being lost, her nerves were on edge anyway.

Amy began to cry quietly.

Bradley asked to be excused.

"I'm sorry. I didn't want to trouble you. We all know I have to go back to school when winter break is over — "

"Then we'll be all alone," Amy whimpered. Her brief sleep had made her cranky instead of rested and Holly wished she had slept through the night as she had anticipated she would.

"No, you won't. You have Honora."

"But, it's not the same," Amy sputtered back.

"I'll be home, again, soon. I thought it better not to mention it until I actually had to go. But, I promise, I'll return on the first train this spring when school is out for the summer."

"Why can't you just stay here," Bradley questioned from the doorway as he was leaving.

"I can't, Bradley. I need to get an education so I can do better things for you and Amy. Papa isn't going to want to support a grown woman for the rest of her life."

"What about Mr. Bingham?" Amy asked.

"Clay?" Holly thought about the future. *Was she really anywhere in Clay's plans?*

"Well, we don't know what Mr. Bingham has in mind for the future, if anything — "

Holly's words trailed off as she felt an instinct of concern gripping her again. *Why hadn't Clay come to the house, yet?*

"Both of you go to bed. I'll be up and tuck you in soon. Go along. Follow Honora and she'll light the lamps for you."

When Holly arrived at Amy's room she pulled the covers up to the little girl's chin and handed her favorite doll to her.

Properly snuggled in and still tired from playing outside in the fresh air, Amy quickly fell back to sleep.

Holly stroked her head and felt her silky blonde curls against her fingers.

"I don't want to go, either, Baby," she whispered so as not to wake the child again.

When she reached Bradley's room, his light was already out and he was a solid lump under the covers. Whether he was really asleep or angry at her, Holly couldn't tell.

The thought of tickling him to see crossed her mind, but she thought better of it. If he was asleep, it would be best. If he wasn't, she would only get him going again with his rampant curiosity.

As she closed his door slightly the light from the wall-mounted lamp threw a glow across his bed. He was safe and sound in his room and she wouldn't have to worry about him for the rest of the night.

She turned down the flame on the wall lamp and went on down the hall toward her own room, She hesitated at the door of the empty room where Clay had slept.

She pushed the door slightly open, knowing she wouldn't be intruding on him. The room was illuminated by the glow of the same style lamp as the one in Bradley's room. Honora had already been there and turned down the bedding.

She wondered if it was a sign he would come in soon.

Holly made her way back downstairs. By the time she reached the last step and put her foot on the thick plush rug atop the polished hardwood floor at the bottom she knew what she would do.

She rushed to the coat closet and grabbed her heaviest cape from inside. Throwing it around her shoulders and pulling it closed in front she called to Honora, "I'm going out, Honora. Don't wait up for me."

CHAPTER TWENTY-ONE

Although the darkness of night had crept into the small town, Holly could see the lights of businesses glowing as she trudged along toward the buildings. Lamps atop tall posts and on the sides near doorways lit the way. Light escaped through uncovered glass windows from interiors to cast broken spots of brightness onto the boardwalk and into the street as far as it could reach.

She had grown up in this community and didn't fear for her safety as she was known by most residents. Still, she hurried along past the open saloons and locked stores toward the Sheriff's Office where a light still showed from its one window near the Sheriff's desk.

When she opened the door, the smell of lamp oil rose swiftly to her nostrils. She saw dark, oily streaks across the rough wood floor where it had soaked into the boards.

A deputy greeted her with surprise.

"Miss O'Flannery! What brings you out here after dark? And alone, I presume."

"I'd like to see the Sheriff."

"He's gone home for the night. He's been putting a lot

of hours in, what with the hotel burning and all."

Holly nodded.

"Well, if he's not here, maybe you can help."

"What can I do for you, Miss Holly?"

"A friend of mine came into town late this afternoon. He had another man with him. I was told they came here."

"You might have been told right, Miss Holly. But, I don't know that I can talk about that."

"Why not? Everybody in town knows they came here. Now, I want to know where Mr. Clay Bingham went afterwards."

"Went? Why, nowhere, Ma'am."

"What do you mean "nowhere"?"

"The Sheriff is holding him here while he investigates a crime."

"What crime?"

"Can't say, Ma'am."

"Then take me to Clay. He'll tell me what's going on, I'm sure."

"Can't do that either, Ma'am. Sheriff said 'no visitors.' I'm sure that means you, too."

The deputy was a young man that had asked to court her a couple of years back. Holly knew she could get him to relent, if she played her cards right.

"Now, Jeremiah, you know I have a right to see my friend."

"Not unless the Sheriff says so, Holly." He dropped his formality.

"How would you like it if I filled the Sheriff in on some of the stunts you pulled before you became his deputy?"

"You wouldn't. Besides, that might be against the law. It sounds like blackmail to me. Sorry, I just can't let you go down the hall unless you bring the Sheriff here or a piece of paper he's written on saying its all right to do so."

While the Deputy knew he couldn't read but few of the words, he would recognize the Sheriff's signature.

"You are one stubborn man, Jeremiah! Maybe that's why I wouldn't let you come calling. Ever think of that?"

She hated resorting to childish tactics but she was unable to budge Jeremiah and she was frustrated.

Without another word, Holly turned on her heel and yanked the door open.

"If I were you, I'd get that oil stink scrubbed up before the Sheriff gets back here."

Jeremiah looked over the top of a wanted poster he fussed with while he evaded her pleas. His eyes met hers. She was mad enough to spit fire and, if he didn't get the fumes out of the office, if and when she managed to bring Charlie back, the sparks in her eyes just might set it into flames.

"Yes, Miss Holly, I'll do that."

Outside, Holly stomped down the boardwalk and took the short path through an unlit field to the Sheriff's home.

Jeremiah had riled her something awful and she was determined she would not go home until she talked to Clay whether Jeremiah liked it or not.

He might have authority while Charlie was out but, once she convinced the Sheriff to go back to his office with her, Jeremiah would have no say, she was sure.

Her cape caught on a dry tumbleweed. She tugged it free and concentrated on the glow in the windows of the Sheriff's house ahead. Somehow she managed to bump her foot into a cat that had crouched nearby at the sound of her footsteps. The animal, as startled as she was ran off, yowling, in another direction. She wondered if there were coyotes roaming about and looked at the sky to see how thick the clouds were covering the shine of the moon.

"Darn cat!" She spoke aloud, "better get home before

the coyotes get you! No thanks for scaring the dickens out of me!"

At last she came to the gate post that attached to the fence which ran around the Sheriff's house. The enclosure was small and simply designated ownership of the lot but did no good at keeping anything out that wanted to get in. She pushed the gate open and walked through. It snapped back with a "bang." She jumped at the sound then, timidly, moved forward.

Before she reached the front porch the Sheriff was standing at the open door with his rifle in his hand.

"Who's out there?" He demanded.

"Me! Holly O'Flannery!"

"My Lord, Miss O'Flannery, what are you doing ramming around out there in the dark? Don't you know it ain't safe to be wandering around somebody's house at night? You coulda got shot!"

Holly stomped up the steps, knocking mud from her boots as she went.

Charlie held the door open for her to go inside and warm up.

"Kate, fix Miss Holly, here, a hot cup of tea, would ya? I imagine it must be something important for her to be out wandering around in the cold and dark this late."

He motioned to Holly. "Let me take your cape."

"It is important, Sheriff. I was just down at the jail and Jeremiah admitted you were holding Clay Bingham. He wouldn't tell me why or let me talk to Clay."

The Sheriff studied Holly as she talked. He didn't admit to anything.

"How do you know this Bingham?"

"Long before you came to work here, Clay and I were young kids and good friends," Holly answered leaving out the part about their romantic interest. "Clay came back to town to clear his name, Sheriff. He isn't the one that killed the Captain. Why, Mr. Collier was everything to Clay. Once his folks were killed he didn't have anybody else but the man who found him. Ask yourself, what would he have to gain by doing that?"

Mrs. Jamison approached with a tray containing a teapot, three cups, a sugar bowl and creamer. They were utilitarian utensils, plain but sturdy without a fancy design of pretentiousness.

The Sheriff and his wife seemed to live simply and she respected that. She'd much prefer to make a home for herself out on a ranch somewhere than live on her father's money. She'd feel better if she could earn her belongings from her own hard work. But, she was sure, not many people would believe that.

"Mrs. Jamison, please, talk some sense into this man! I've known Clay for years. He came into town riding through bad weather and good to go to school. He never complained one bit about it. Or, about any of his troubles that led to him losing his home and family."

"I'm sorry, Holly, I can't tell the Sheriff how to do his job. I'm sure, if he's got someone locked up, he has good reason."

Charlie sat back and listened to the two women talk.

Finally, he reached for his hat that sat nearby on a table.

"All I can tell you is he was pointed out as Captain Collier's killer a few years ago. I have to keep him confined until I get the answers I need. He'll see the Circuit Court Judge the next time he comes to town. If he says I got nothing to hold him on, then, I'll have to let him go."

"But, Sheriff, that could take days."

"Maybe a couple weeks. He's due in here once a month, but sometimes, he gets delayed."

"Clay would never have killed the Captain or anybody

else, for that matter. He appreciated what the Colliers did for him."

"Well, I guess it wouldn't do any harm to let you see him for a few minutes. Besides, it does me good to know Jeremiah couldn't be swayed to give up information by a pretty young lady. And, I bet you tried, too." He winked at his wife.

"I'll be home shortly," Jamison told his wife as he went to the door.

Mrs. Jamison helped Holly put on her cloak.

"Thank you for your hospitality Mrs. Jamison," Holly said as she went out the door the Sheriff held open for her.

"Be careful, Dear," Mrs. Jamison said.

Holly didn't know if her comment was aimed at her, her husband or both of them.

CHAPTER TWENTY-TWO

When Holly and the Sheriff reached his office, Jeremiah sat tilted back in the desk chair with a cup of coffee balanced on the knee of his outstretched leg. He jumped up at the sound of the door opening, tipping the cup. It fell to the floor but surprisingly did not break. Hot coffee scalded his leg through his pants. Jeremiah brushed rapidly at the spilled hot drink that was soaking his pants' leg.

Holly noticed a heavy smell of lye soap and sensed Jeremiah had taken her suggestion seriously and scrubbed, or had someone else attempt to scrub, the oil stain from the floor.

"Quiet night, Sheriff," Jeremiah told him half in defense of his guard being down. "With those two fellers separated by a couple of empty cells, I hain't heard much outta them."

"I hope you checked to see if they were both still there," Charlie said.

"Oh, sure. The Bingham fellow's been lying on the bunk. T'other one's been pacing the floor like he wanted to get out but couldn't figure out how."

The Sheriff reached for the key ring to unlock the door

173

that opened to the hall where the cells were located.

Holly was right on his heels as he moved.

Clay rose from the cot when the door opened, throwing light into the cell.

"Clay!" Holly spoke as she rushed to the cell door.

"Holly, what are you doing here?"

"I've come to try and put some sense about you into the Sheriff's head," Holly looked at the Sheriff with a scathing stare.

"Now, Holly," Charlie cautioned her.

"Sorry, Sheriff. It's just that I know Clay would never do anything like you're accusing him of."

"And," Clay started as the Sheriff turned his back to leave. "Wait, Sheriff! I've been laying here thinking how we could prove I didn't do it."

"Oh? And how might that be?"

"Take me back to your desk, I'll show you."

"My desk? What does that have to do with anything?"

"Clay, what are you saying?" Holly was as puzzled as the Sheriff. She looked at Clay as he waited for the Sheriff's answer.

"What would it hurt, Sheriff? If Clay can prove his innocence, why not give him this one request?" Holly pleaded.

"Well, I guess it won't hurt. Jeremiah's still here to help if you decided to try to make a break for it. You don't have a derringer in that cloak of yours, do you Miss Holly?"

"Of course not, Sheriff! Whatever would make you think I'd try to help someone make a jail break? Besides, you're the one that hung my cape up when I got to your house. That idea is just — just — ridiculous!"

"Never can be too careful," Charlie told her.

It was clear that Holly was insulted, but Clay got his way. The Sheriff unlocked the jail cell and led them toward his desk.

"Sit down, both of you," he ordered as though he trusted no one. "Bolt the door, Jeremiah."

"Look, Sheriff, I knew the Captain very well. I bet those saddlebags you got in the safe belonged to him. They were probably full of cash when he was killed. The killer wouldn't have hung around and transferred the money into something else, now, would he?"

"I don't know. But, I doubt it. He sure wouldn't want to get caught like the local fellas said you were."

"I was bringing the Captain's body in," Clay repeated in exasperation.

"Anyway the Captain had a strange habit of marking everything he owned. He'd had a blacksmith make him a tiny branding iron with the ranch brand on it. The mark it made wasn't but about the size of a two-bit piece. He could brand things in the tightest places. I've seen him do it by heating the iron over a candle flame when he wanted to mark the back of a leather-bound book."

The Sheriff looked interested.

"But, even if they are branded, who's to say you didn't leave them there at the hotel anyway?"

"Because mine are on my horse, right now. Which I hope you have had taken to the stable instead of leaving to freeze in the street."

"You're horse is safe. But, there's still the question of whether those are the Captain's property. And, if they are, who left them at the hotel."

"Not Clay. Clay was at my house the night before the hotel caught fire, Sheriff," Holly said without hesitation.

Jamison looked surprised.

Holly didn't want him to get the wrong idea about what had gone on at the house.

"Amy had an accident and nearly drowned. Clay saved

175

her life. I insisted he stay and get dried out after he took us home. I wasn't going to be inhospitable when he revived Amy! We nearly lost her, Sheriff! If it wasn't for Clay, we would have! At least, can't you look for the mark, Sheriff," Holly finally asked. "Besides, wouldn't it look strange if Clay was dragging two sets of saddlebags all over the place? I can vouch for him having his with him at my house. For God's sake, he saved Amy's life, Sheriff!" She said as if that would exonerate Clay.

The Sheriff rose and went to the safe. He returned with the saddlebags and held them above the desk. He spun them slowly from the middle of the leather that held the two together and would straddle the horse while a rider was in transit.

"I don't see a mark anywhere," he stated flatly. "I'd like to believe you and Miss Holly. But, as you see, there is nothing here."

"The Captain wouldn't have made it that obvious," Clay said. "Take the things out and look inside," Clay suggested.

Carefully the Sheriff removed the items inside.

"Jeremiah, would you hold that lamp over here so I can get a good look?"

Jeremiah complied. The Sheriff angled the inside of each bag so he could see the interior clearly.

"Nope, nothing there either." He started to return the jacket and other evidence inside.

"Wait," Holly cried out. "You said he often would conceal the mark, didn't you Clay?"

"Yes."

"Well, look at the seam inside, Sheriff." Holly wanted to jerk the bags from the Sheriff's hand and look for herself, but she fought the urge. *What if Clay was wrong? What if there was no mark? Even so, how did they prove it wasn't him that left them at the hotel? The Sheriff had only their*

176

word for that.

The Sheriff was tiring of their attempts to convince him to free Clay. He knew, at the very least, he would have to keep him overnight until he could see the Justice of the Peace the next morning. Then, probably, still hold him for the Circuit Judge.

Along the sides and across the bottom of each saddlebag the Sheriff found a half-inch seam on both bags where the material had been sewn when they were made.

He ran his fingers along the seam and felt leather that had been worn smooth by the contents carried inside.

He looked up, ready to give Clay and Holly the bad news.

As he opened his mouth, a surprised look came across his face.

Where the seam came together in the corner he felt something different. His fingers touched a strange roughness. He grabbed the seam and turned the bag inside out. There was the tiniest brand he had ever seen. Seared into the material was a circle with two capitol "C"s connected in the center. The edges of the leather around the letters showed rougher than the smooth burn of the brand.

"This what you're talking about?" He asked Clay.

"Yes, Sir!" Clay's voice carried an excited ring to it. "That's it! I asked the Captain one time how those two Cs managed to look like there was nothing to hold them together. He explained that there was a bar that went across the back but not all the way to the front. So, when he pressed the iron down, he got a clear image of the Circle Two Cs. I began to notice, the brands on the cattle were the same. I never thought about it before that."

"Does this mean I can take Clay home with me, Sheriff?" Holly asked as if the answer were a given.

"No. Wait a minute. There's still the question of who left the bags at the hotel."

"Well, it wasn't me. You know I didn't rob the bank because too many people saw who did. Nearly everybody in town saw Simmons wear that coat."

"I'm still going to have to keep you over night until I talk to the Justice of the Peace."

Clay stiffened.

The Sheriff returned the saddlebags to the safe. He jangled the keys and motioned for Clay to return to the cell.

"I'll give you two a few minutes, then, see to it that Miss Holly gets back to her home safely." He turned toward his desk to give them some privacy. When he reached his chair and sat down, he spoke quietly to his deputy.

"I've got some paperwork to finish up here, Jeremiah. Will you walk Miss Holly home? I'll wait until you return before making my rounds and going home myself."

CHAPTER TWENTY-THREE

"I better go," Holly told Clay. She didn't want to stall and have the Sheriff become uncooperative.

Clay reached through the woven lattice door of the cell and took her hand. He kissed her fingers. He had no words that would ease her concern. This was the last place he wanted to be, but neither he, nor she, could do anything about it.

"I think we better try to stay on the Sheriff's good side," Holly said. "Clay, you know I love you even though we haven't talked about how we felt since your return." *Was she taking a risk saying those words before she heard them from his lips?* She wondered.

"There's never been the proper time to tell you, Holly. I wanted to, but I — I guess I was just too shy to say anything real serious. Now, who knows what will happen. You have to know I love you, too. If all this doesn't go well, I wouldn't want to be convicted and leave you wondering."

Holly dipped her chin to her chest so Clay wouldn't see her tears. She didn't want to think of what might lay ahead for him. Clay lifted her chin with his fingertips.

"I left you wondering once. I promised I would never do it again if it was within my power. No matter what happens, being apart from you is not something I will do of my own choice."

"I'll come back first thing in the morning. I'll bring you some of Honora's corn fritter cakes and syrup for breakfast."

"Try to come up with something to tell Bradley and Amy that doesn't sound so terrible. I'm not asking you to lie to them. Maybe you can find some easier way to satisfy their curiosity."

Clay stroked the tears from her cheeks.

"Go, now. We both have a busy day ahead of us tomorrow," he told her.

Holly drew her cape closer around her. Before she reached the outer room, Jeremiah put his hat on and pulled the front door open.

Holly hesitated.

"I asked Jeremiah to see you safely home," the Sheriff told her. She was surprised that it wouldn't be the Sheriff, himself, walking her to her house but kept her comments to herself.

"Goodnight, Sheriff."

"Goodnight, Holly. Maybe we'll have better news for you tomorrow."

Holly locked eyes with him momentarily then went out into the cold night air with Jeremiah following behind her.

They walked in silence down the boardwalk toward her home.

Loud music and boisterous conversation came from inside one of the saloons when they passed by.

Holly felt uneasy walking with Jeremiah. He had wanted to be a suitor and gotten upset when she turned him down. She knew, at the time, he was particularly jealous of her choice of Clay over him when they were younger. She hoped he would be a gentleman and do his duty without causing her any problems.

A drunken man staggered down the boardwalk toward them. His features dimly lit by the light from inside the Silver Bar Saloon coming through a dirty window she, at first, didn't recognize him.

Jeremiah got between her and the angle the man appeared to be staggering.

"Pa!"

The man looked at her with blurry, unseeing eyes and unhearing ears. He staggered past to the next saloon.

"Let's get you to the house, Holly," Jeremiah told her.

"Yes," she answered. There'd be time later to deal with this additional problem. With her father back in town, helping Clay could be compromised or, at least, more difficult.

They were off the boardwalk, now, and traversing the soggy road where the night's cold was beginning to freeze the day's snow melt in the mud.

Jeremiah took Holly's elbow in order to keep her upright if her boots slipped on the forming ice.

She could see the lights still lit in the house and wanted, desperately, to get inside where it was warm and safe. The sooner she was out of Jeremiah's grasp, literally, the happier she would be. She would deal with her father when he sobered up again. Even though she hadn't expected him back from Europe so soon, he never failed to keep her in the dark where his plans were concerned.

It was a wonder he hadn't fallen overboard on the trip, Holly thought. She couldn't imagine he might have given up drinking which had become a natural order of things for him. To drink all night and sleep most of the day before getting up to do it all over again had been his way of life for as long as she could remember. She didn't want to let her mind go there, back to the early days when his drunkenness first started. So, she turned to Jeremiah.

"Of course, you know that was my father," she said matter-of-factly.

"Yes. The Sheriff has had me put him in a cell to sober up more than once." His voice carried a tone of dislike to her ears.

"I'm sorry he made such a spectacle of himself."

As they approached the front entrance of the house, she saw Jeremiah shrug in the glow of the entry light as if it was no concern of his.

Holly reached for the door knob before Jeremiah's hand clasped it. His palm landed, instead, on top of hers — and stayed there.

She looked up at him.

Taking her hand from the knob, he pulled her toward him.

"What are you doing, Jeremiah?" Holly demanded.

"You know how I feel about you, Holly. All this way, I've wanted to take your hand or encircle your shoulders with my arm. Not just steady you by your elbow hidden beneath your cape."

"I thought I made myself clear, Jeremiah. I'm not interested in courting you."

"Oh, you did, for certain. But, that doesn't stop my feeling how I do about you."

"Jeremiah!" Holly nearly squealed as he pulled her tight to him and kissed her hard on the mouth cutting off the barrage of words that would have come after his name.

Holly shoved him, hard, slamming his back against one of the marble columns holding the entry roof overhead.

"What is the matter with you? Isn't it enough you've got Clay in jail? And, now, my father is back at the worst of all times? Get away from me! And, keep away," Holly sputtered. She shoved the front door open and slammed it closed behind her. She latched the locking hasp of the door to its counterpart on the doorframe. Still shaking, she steadied herself with her back against the solid door while her knees shook and threatened to let her body slide to the floor. She squeezed her eyes tight and scrubbed the back of her hand across her lips. She held her breath and listened. When she didn't hear Jeremiah outside anymore, she opened her eyes to look around for reassurance she was truly safe.

In front of her, exposed by the dim light of the dying fireplace coals were bundles and trunks strewn around blocking her way across the room.

Her father was home, for sure! It hadn't been an illusion she had seen on the boardwalk. The clutter and disarray made it real for her.

CHAPTER TWENTY-FOUR

The next morning Ian O'Flannery had not returned from the saloons to his own house.

Holly requested the corn cakes from Honora. She saw that the children were fed while dodging their incessant questions about the bundles in the living room. She prepared herself to go to the jail with plenty of food to start Clay's day.

When she arrived on the Sheriff's Office steps, she could hear voices and saw people inside through the window. She edged the door open carefully in order to squeeze herself into the small crowded space.

"Oh, Miss Holly," Sheriff Charlie Jamison said somewhat surprised at her arrival. "You're here early!"

"No doubt a surprise to your deputy, too!" Holly said but didn't explain herself. She shot an angry look at Jeremiah.

He ducked his head and busied himself with loading wood into the pot-bellied stove to avoid a direct verbal attack he felt was coming.

"I've asked Tyler Washington to join us here. You do

know Mr. Washington, don't you, Holly?"

"Good Morning, Mr. Washington," she acknowledged the banker as she nodded her head "yes."

"I've asked him here to identify the bank robber that robbed his bank. I'll have to ask you to wait a bit with the food until he does that."

"Certainly," she agreed.

"It won't take long, I guarantee it."

"I didn't get a good look at the fellow when he was in the bank cause he had his face covered. So, I don't know if I'll be able to tell right off which one did it," Washington said to anyone interested.

Holly looked at the Sheriff with curiosity. *Surely, they all knew it wasn't Clay.*

Charlie shook his head to warn her not to comment.

She complied with difficulty.

While the Sheriff and Washington stepped to the back, Holly waited, setting the basket of food on the desk.

Jeremiah clattered the lid on the stove top noisily as he shoved the metal plate with a handle back across the open hole where the wood burned beneath the surface. He put on his hat, tipped it to Holly and, sheepishly, walked outside.

The Sheriff and Mr. Washington returned.

Holly looked up.

"Between the two, it has to be that Simmons fellow, all right," Washington said. "I barely knew him when he stayed at the hotel. But he's taller than the other fellow. Funny, I had breakfast with the both of 'em and never would have thought one of them would rob me."

Holly sensed a ray of hope.

"That still doesn't prove he was the one to kill Collier," Charlie said.

"My guess would be he was," Washington said.

The Sheriff stood quietly in thought.

"Holly, you go ahead and take breakfast in, if you want."

She would rather stay there and hear their discussion but lifted the basket instead and headed down the hall.

"I tend to believe that, too," Charlie told Washington in a quieter voice. "There's enough evidence to take him to court. But, unless we can get a confession out of him or see what someone else has to say about Bingham's story, I still have to question Bingham's part in all this."

"I understand. Well, at least my customers will get some of their money back. But, you probably noticed, some of the numbers on the larger bills didn't match the ones on the list."

"Yep. I saw that. Made me curious."

"Well, I did some checking at the bank and that was because they matched numbers on some of the bills I gave Collier when he came to town that day wanting cash for his cattle purchase."

"That certainly digs a deeper hole for Simmons, I'd say," Charlie replied.

"Sure looks that way. That's why I said I'd almost bet he did it. If I was a betting man. Why else would the money be in the saddle bags? He musta got scared off when you showed up when the hotel caught fire. Probably was scared to go in after 'em," Tyler Washington said.

"Don't know if he was afraid I'd catch him or that he'd get trapped in the burning building. Either way, if he had the bags, he must be the one that killed Collier. It looks like he was the owner of that jacket. So, circumstantial evidence or not, it sure sounds like he's our man," Charlie replied.

"As soon as Jeremiah or my other deputy gets back in here, I'm going to take a ride out to the Collier spread and poke around. See what I can find out. When I get back, I'll question Simmons some more. Maybe I can put him in a position to put it in writing."

"I better get the bank opened," Washington said. "Folks will be glad to hear you have a suspect in the robbery caught, too," he added with cheeriness in his voice. "Customer Service," he said lightheartedly. "That's what it's all about."

"I wish my job was as easy as yours," Charlie jibed him as he left to open the bank for the day.

Charlie walked to the cell where Clay picked at his corn cakes. Holly stood on the outside of the cell watching as though she wished Clay would eat more heartily.

"Where's my grub, Sheriff," Simmons called from the far cell.

"It'll be here in a minute. Mrs. Swanson promised she'd go ahead and send her boy down with a plate as soon as she could get it done." He turned to Holly, "She's trying to get used to the kitchen over at the Red Dog Saloon. Got a job there cooking while they figure out what to do about the hotel. Guess the boy got sick and couldn't take the trip. Old man Swanson sent him back from their hunting trip early. He thought he was going to crawl into a warm bed until he rode in and saw what happened to their building. Him and the younger Swanson boy are bunking out in the hay at the livery for now."

"Sheriff," Holly asked wanting to get right to Clay's situation, "you said Clay would be seeing the Justice of the Peace this morning. What time is that?"

"Well, I was going to take him to the courthouse as soon as the Justice was in."

"Was?" Clay and Holly both echoed. The sooner they could get him out of jail, the better. They both were of the same mind.

"Yep, but I decided I better postpone that until I gather some more evidence."

Clay looked at the Sheriff and handed his plate back to

Holly. *That could indicate good news or bad news for him.*
Either way, he wasn't sure he liked the sound of it.

~*~

Sheriff Jamison left town near lunch time and rode to
the Collier Ranch. He tied his horse in front at the hitching
rail and made no pretense of surprising Marguerite Collier.

Still, when she opened the door to his knock, she
seemed shocked to see him.

"Why, Sheriff, what are you doing way out here?"

"This isn't a social call, Maggie. I need to talk to you."

"Certainly, come on in. I've got some fresh coffee on the
stove. Would you like a cup?"

The Sheriff removed his hat without answering.

"Pull up a chair. I'll pour you a cup."

Charlie Jamison sat down. He crossed one leg over the
other and dropped the crown of his hat over the upper
knee. He wasn't sure how to approach the woman with the
questions he had.

"You know the Captain and I went way back," he
started.

"Yes, I understood that when I came here."

"Funny as well as we knew each other he never once
told me anything about you."

"Guess there wasn't much to tell."

"Not if he didn't know anything about your past."

"My past?" Maggie asked as she sat the cup of black
coffee before him in a heavy porcelain mug and offered him
the cream pitcher and sugar bowl.

He waved his hand across the cup. "No, just black is
fine."

"I don't know what "past" you are talking about,
Sheriff."

"Well, I've got a fellow in jail in town that says
different."

"What? What are you trying to say, Sheriff?"

"Says he's your son, Maggie."

"Then, he's a liar," Maggie turned away and poked at the wood inside the cook stove through a drop-down door.

"That could be. Just the same, I need to take you back to town with me to have a talk."

"But, I've got things to do here today."

"If we get this all cleared up, I'll see to it you get back home as quickly as possible."

"You're not drinking your coffee, Sheriff," Maggie said accusingly.

"I don't believe I care to. Now, ring that dinner triangle out there until one of your hands comes up. Have him hitch up your buggy. We're going to town."

CHAPTER TWENTY-FIVE

The Collier buggy entered Main Street with Sheriff
Jamison behind the reins and Mrs. Collier sitting solemnly
beside him. His horse trailed behind, led by a rope clipped to
its bridle and tied to a ring at the back of the buggy.

Charlie was taking no chances that Maggie Collier might
attempt to break away from him if she were driving the
buggy and sitting alone at the reins. It would have been a
foolish action on her part and they both knew it. But,
desperation could lead to foolish things. He'd seen it do so
in the past.

Charlie slowed the buggy as they reached the
congestion of wagons and horses three blocks away from his
office.

He wondered why the town was abuzz with people and
conveyances. Anyone that didn't wave as they rode by,
stared to see who the Sheriff had with him.

Maggie slipped as far back in the seat as she could
hoping to shelter her profile with the buggy cover that was
designed to keep the weather off its passengers.

She hadn't spoken a word the whole trip and Charlie

suspected that she was trying to refine her alibi, if she was, indeed, guilty of the accusations. He had been cautioned more than once about ignoring the old dictum that someone was "innocent until proven guilty."

"Just sit tight until I tie the horses to the hitching rail. If need be, I'll have the Swanson boy come put them in the livery."

"And what might make you do that?" Maggie Collier asked.

"You never know. Might need to get them out of the weather," Charlie replied. *Or,* he thought, *the answers you give to my questions might be cause to arrest you.*

Charlie returned to where Maggie sat. He reached up to assist her down. When he grasped her by her wrist instead of taking her hand in his, she jerked away.

He'd intended to keep her in his grasp.

She still searched for a way out of her situation.

She stepped over the low panel on the side of the buggy and caught her dress on a bolt, tossing her forward and toward the ground where she would have landed if Charlie hadn't caught her. Once she was on her feet she glared at Charlie for a second before balancing herself and taking a step forward.

Charlie stood aside to let her walk ahead of him where he'd be aware of her every move.

"Up the steps and into my office, Mrs. Collier," he directed but didn't move to guide her by the elbow. "Watch your step. Never know when you're going to trip going up."

Maggie stiffened her back and stepped solidly on each of the two narrow boards.

When Charlie opened the door for her and she went inside, he called to a deputy, "Jeremiah, I need you to go get a clerk from the courthouse. Get a stenographer that can take down notes word for word," he directed.

Holly nearly bumped into Maggie Collier as she came out of the hall from Clay's cell to return home from bringing him his lunch.

"Hello," Holly spoke with surprise.

Maggie stretched a false smile across her taut lips.

"I was just gathering my things to leave, Sheriff. I'll be out of you way in a minute." She quickly dropped the red and white checkered gingham napkin across the dishes in the wicker basket and removed it from the desk. She brushed at any crumbs that might be left.

"Please, have a seat Mrs. Collier," Charlie said, pulling the one wooden straight-backed chair over in front of his desk and rolling his larger chair where he could face her directly when he sat down.

He removed his hat.

"Would you like to take your wraps off?" He asked Maggie.

She shook her head and clutched the long heavy winter coat tight to her body.

"Very well," he said, "then we'll just wait for Jeremiah to get back here with a clerk."

~*~

With Jeremiah gone, and despite her curiosity, Holly left also. She sensed the Sheriff wouldn't let her stay and she didn't want to deal with the possibility of Jeremiah being instructed to see here home, again, even in broad daylight.

There was nothing she and Clay could do now, but wait. And waiting was difficult.

Whatever business the Sheriff had with Mrs. Collier was none of her business, she told herself. She certainly didn't want to discuss Clay's situation with the widow of the man he was accused of killing.

On the way back to her house her mind was busy with other problems in her life that were interwoven with Clay.

Ian O'Flannery was back and her independence could easily be cramped. Especially if her father was sober enough to know what was going on in town.

Alone she felt safer than with Jeremiah, who was, yet, another problem, all be it a minor one. Thinking back to the moments before Jeremiah left the Sheriff's Office she remembered he had offered to send for the other deputy so he could run the errand the Sheriff wanted him to do instead. She thought, now, he must have been plotting a way so he would be free to walk her home as before. Even without the Sheriff's direction, he offered to walk with her on the way to complete the Sheriff's bidding.

"No, thank you," she had said emphatically. "It is daylight, there is no need."

Jeremiah had only shrugged and, knowing he had been out of line before, didn't press the issue.

Holly didn't know what she could have expected had he gotten his way and been her companion on the walk back home. Surely, he wouldn't try anything in broad daylight! But, then, she couldn't be sure. After the last instance, she felt a fear that went beyond being uncomfortable in his company.

~*~

When she entered the house she quickly sat the basket on a chair in the kitchen.

Honora turned from a work table where she had been kneading bread dough.

"Mr. came home a couple of hours ago. I suspect he'll be sleeping most of the day, now," she said with the slightest tinge of contempt in her voice.

"Yes, I suppose," Holly answered with distraction. She was so used to her father's pattern and so worried about Clay, she only half heard Honora's words.

"The children are in the library working on their lessons.

I gave them both instructions and left them to do them. I haven't heard a peep out of either one of them since. So, they must be working hard. I promised them a caramel crisp for lunch if they finished in time."

"Thank you, Honora, I'll check on them as I pass the library. Bradley can be a sneaky little stinker about fooling us with his lessons when he wants to."

"Yes," Honora agreed. "I have had to remove his toys and insist he get back to his desk and do his sums."

When Holly entered the main living room, she saw that someone, probably Honora, had neatened the trunks, luggage and containers and pushed them against the wall. She had probably asked Joshua to help her and to stack them out of the way against the wall as they were all, now, away from the center of the room. At last, one could easily traverse the rug without falling over the mess.

It hadn't occurred to Holly to be curious about what all the cartons contained. Only whether she would find her father sprawled across the jumbled assembly if she had chosen to enter by the front instead of the side door into the kitchen.

Honora was right. As she passed the library, there was not a sound between the two children. She was pleased. Obviously, they were minding Honora well. She considered it was probably because of the promise of a treat later.

She went on up to her room and put away her outerwear in exchange for a less constricting dress to move about the house more freely.

Sometimes being wealthy had its inconveniences. One was dressing respectably in public. She could hear her father snoring down the hall. A slight chill went through her body. *How was she going to manage him when he found out Clay was in town? Not only in town, but had slept in his house? And, now, was in jail?* She searched for an answer as she prepared to look for something undone to give her busy work and keep her mind off her problems.

CHAPTER TWENTY-SIX

Holly passed the door to the library once more on her way to ask Honora if she could use her assistance with anything. She tip-toed quietly past the opening noting that the door was slid into its pocket giving open access to the room. She listened intently. She heard nothing. Not the sound of a page turning nor a whispered word.

She couldn't believe the two children would be so engrossed in their schoolwork that they wouldn't be aware of her peering into the room regardless of how quiet she was. Bradley, especially, usually seemed to look for an excuse to set his studies aside. Holly stepped forward and peered into the large room lined with tall bookcases. Two small desks were positioned near her father's larger desk. A round library table with books spread open on top filled the center of the room.

She observed everything that was there. Everything was in order. Except — there were no children. Bradley and Amy definitely were absent from their desks. Neither child was working on their papers as they should have been.

"Bradley! Amy!" Holly called. When she got no answer,

she called out to Honora, "Honora, are the children in there with you?"

Honora came to the kitchen archway, wiping the remains of bread dough from her fingers onto her white apron.

"No. They should be in the library."

"But, they're not!" Holly was becoming alarmed. "Where could they be?"

Honora rushed to the empty room. She bent to pick up Amy's stick-figure drawing. She looked into the kneehole space of the first desk. She looked into the open space where Bradley's legs should be under his desk and, finally, into the blank space of the larger adult-sized desk as well.

There were no children anywhere.

Holly ran through the house calling their names. No one answered.

Honora went to the closet beside the entry. There she searched for the children's outer gear they wore when playing outside. All of it was gone except one of Amy's small pink mittens.

"Miss Holly, I did not give them permission to go outside. They had work to do. I would have felt the day was too cold, yet, had they asked to go."

"Well, obviously they didn't bother to ask and went anyway. Bradley probably knew the answer would be "no" if he had come to you about it."

Honora resorted to her native tongue and rattled off a long comment which Holly wasn't too sure didn't contain a few swear words.

Holly didn't understand if Honora's rapid spurt of Spanish was a deluge of words about how much trouble the children were or a prayer that they would be found safe.

"They must be out in the yard playing," Holly said hopefully.

"Of course. I am sure that is the case," Honora spoke English again.

But, even though both women went to search for them, they were nowhere to be found. Not in the yard or in the stable when Honora rushed to check with Joshua.

She returned with Joshua hurrying behind her.

"What are we to do, Miss Holly?" Joshua asked.

"We have to find them. They'll freeze out here in this temperature. Amy can't walk too far on her little legs and Bradley certainly wouldn't be able to carry her."

"I'll take a horse and see if I can track them," Joshua said. "Four small footprints should leave a trail easy enough to follow. Don't worry, Miss Holly. We'll find them."

Holly rushed back inside and bundled up for her own search.

"You stay here, Honora, in case they come back home first. They'll probably be cold and hungry. I'm going to go toward town and see if I can find them."

As Holly left the front porch she realized Bradley's sled, that she had told him time and again to put away, was missing. She was sure he had not followed her orders because he was in bed the last time she reminded him. He wouldn't have gotten out of bed and done it then. Or, as she reasoned, have remembered to do it this morning when it wasn't on its hook next to the outside wall by the kitchen door. She remembered, distinctly, telling herself to remind him again when she came home and saw the hook still empty. Yet, there were no marks where the sled had been pulled through the shallow snow in the yard.

Footprints were marked on top of each other alongside the path leading to the gate and, although they were scuffed through the snow, she knew they had to be those of the children.

She wrapped a wool scarf up over her head and around

her ears and started out. She would have liked to stuff her hands in her pockets but, afraid of slipping on the icy path, she wanted her hands free to catch herself if she started to fall.

Once she was a few feet outside the gate she saw where the sled had been placed in the snow and, as she walked, realized the impression was deeper than the empty sled would probably make. There must be more weight on the sled. The footprints had gone from two in Bradley's size and two smaller ones to only those that might be Bradley's.

Chances were Bradley was pulling Amy wherever they were headed. She knew Amy could be cranky if she got cold. She had been known to refuse to take one more step when she was in an obstinate mood. Bradley knew that, too. *That was probably why he decided to take the sled,* Holly reasoned.

The tracks of the sled appeared to be heading toward the buildings on the main road. Taking the small conveyance into heavy traffic there was dangerous. Aside from startling horses and riders, two small children might not be visible alongside a large wagon or the stagecoach.

Holly hurried. She listened for a commotion in the direction the sled appeared to be traveling. She prayed the children would be safe while she rushed toward the buildings where she was sure she would find them.

At last, Holly saw Amy sitting on the sled with her back to her. Bradley, facing away from her, pulled the sled by its rope to drag his sister over the rough ruts and chunks of ice near the burned-out hotel.

"Bradley! Amy!" Holly yelled to them.

They kept going.

Either they didn't hear her or pretended not to. Bradley seemed intent on getting somewhere.

She hoped it wasn't to the hotel he had been so blasted

curious about.

But, he moved on by with only a few glances at the devastation.

By the time Holly caught up to them and flew past Amy to grab Bradley by the coat they were halfway down what served as a street nearly to the Sheriff's Office.

"What do you think you are doing, Bradley O'Flannery?" Holly demanded.

Bradley turned with her jerk of his coat to look into her face.

Amy started crying.

"He made me come, Holly. I told him it was cold. But, he promised we'd get candy."

"Pull that thing off to the side, Bradley," Holly demanded as she gathered Amy up into her arms and stepped onto the boardwalk. "And stay out of the way of people trying to get by."

Bradley looked down and waited for Holly's fury to pass.

"Pa flipped me a coin this morning when he came in." He dug in his coat pocket and held the proof up to Holly's face. "I wanted to go to the store and get something with it. I was going to share by getting some candy for the both of us."

It's not about sharing, Bradley! It's about you and your sister getting hurt. You could have been killed. There's too much foot traffic, too many horses. And, what about the freight wagons? Why, they're passing right by here to the train depot all the time. You nearly scared me to death!"

Amy whimpered in Holly's arms. Holly sat her on her feet on the boardwalk.

"You pick that thing up and carry it for now, Bradley," she said pointing at the sled.

"We'll go to the store but you are going to buy your sister some candy and give me whatever money is left. You get nothing because you put the both of you in danger. Understand?"

"Yes, Holly," Bradley pouted.

When they reached the General Store Holly instructed Bradley to leave the sled behind an empty barrel outside the door while they went inside.

"But, what if somebody buys it?" Bradley worried.

"Then good riddance. You won't have it to get into trouble with anymore."

To Holly's dismay, the sled was still there when they came out of the store. She decided to utilize it rather than try to pack Amy all the way home.

She walked the children to an alley and situated the two of them on the sled with Bradley behind his sister. Then she tugged the sled down the alley and onto another makeshift lane where the traffic was lighter. She knew it would be easier to avoid anyone who decided to ride down Second Street, such as it was.

At last, they crossed the main street at the end of town and went back onto their own property.

She let Amy and Bradley up and watched them run toward the porch. Amy, she knew, wanted to be inside where she could warm up and eat her candy.

Bradley probably hoped to escape more punishment.

"Bradley!" Holly called. "Come back here and put this sled on its hook where it belongs. And, don't ever take it and go anywhere unless I tell you that you can!"

"Yes, Holly," he begrudgingly agreed.

"And when you are finished, go apologize to Honora for worrying her so much before you do your schoolwork."

"Ah, Holly, do I have to do the schoolwork? I'm tired after all the walking and riding."

"Yes! Maybe, next time you won't get any ideas about leaving it undone and taking off on your own adventure."

She would have to have a talk with her father about giving the children so much money even though she knew it would do no good. He probably didn't even remember doing it if he was in one of his drunken hazes.

She would put the change up for Bradley for later when she felt he had learned his lesson.

She wasn't sure how long that would take.

CHAPTER TWENTY-SEVEN

Jeremiah returned to the Sheriff's Office with the only available clerk at his side. He rolled a small round of cottonwood up close to the desk and upended it. He offered the young man with a couple of pencils between his fingers, and a pad of lined paper under his arm, a place to sit.

The clerk laid his tools on the desk top, looking at the Sheriff for approval. Then, removed his coat and stretched his arms forward to ready himself for the task.

"Now, Jeremiah, you're my witness so stay right here and listen good. When we're finished I'm going to want you to sign that what is written down is the truth as you heard it."

Jeremiah nodded.

"But, Charlie," he said in nearly a whisper of confidence, "you know I can't — "

Charlie broke him off.

"I know. We'll figure that out when we're finished."

"Now, Maggie, tell me your full name, please." He looked at the clerk to be sure he was ready to write.

The clerk wiggled his pencil in the air and pulled the pad

of paper beneath it.

"You know my name, Charlie Jamison."

"Yes, I know it. But I want this all written down as a legal document. So, give the boy your name like I asked."

When Maggie still hesitated, he repeated the "please."

"Marguerite Collier."

The clerk looked up at the Sheriff with a questioning gaze.

"Spell your first name for the boy, Maggie," Charlie said.

"M-a-r-g-u-e-r-i-t-e. Most folks call me Maggie. M-a-g-g-i-e," she looked at the clerk with disdain as if to humble him.

"The boy can spell "Maggie" or he wouldn't be working for the Justice of the Peace," Charlie assured her.

She looked away and contemplated what she would say as the questions came her way.

"Your age?"

"None of your business."

"Put down 45, that ought to be close enough."

Maggie scoffed.

"Asking a lady her age! What's become of men these days?"

"How long had you and the Captain been married, before he was killed, I mean?"

"Nearly twelve years."

"And in all that time, did you ever tell him you'd been married before?"

Maggie pursed her lips and refused to answer.

"Ever tell him you had a boy?"

Again, she refused to answer.

The clerk looked at the Sheriff questioningly.

"Well, if you don't want to answer, I'll tell you what I know. I did a lot of research. And I don't think you're going to like what you hear. But it's the truth. Leastwise, as the Sheriff over in Dodge City filled me in by telegraph. What he left out, I found out from a reliable witness that knew the Captain for most of his life. Hell, he even served with him during the Civil War."

Maggie stared straight ahead.

"Men at war together, get pretty close, Marguerite Hollingsworth Simmons Collier."

Maggie shot a surprised look at the Sheriff.

"Be sure to write all this down," he told the clerk. "We'll fill in the names of the witness and the Dodge City Sheriff when we're finished."

The clerk prepared to write rapidly as the Sheriff's tone indicated he might be required to do.

"As most of us know, the Captain was a Union officer. Once the war was over, he met Maggie, here, in Dodge City.

By now Maggie had had enough. "No man but my husband calls me that! You, Sir, will address me as Marguerite!"

"Fine. Marguerite was known there as Cattle Maggie. Her and her first husband teamed up with some cattle thieves out of Mexico. They set up to sell beef to the military, didn't matter which side or whose cattle it was."

Maggie fidgeted in her chair.

"They paid the rustlers to round up other folks cattle and herd them to a spread they were squatting on out of range of either side. Some, they say, came from as far away as across the border with Mexico where other rustlers had already corralled them up nice and tight."

"Once the law got wind of what they were doing, a posse rode in to stop it. Her husband and most of the rustlers were killed. What ones did survive or were wounded took off to Mexico."

"The posse rounded the cattle up and saw to it most folks got back as many head as they'd lost — even if it wasn't their own animals. They had a legal piece of paper that gave them title to the livestock."

"Maggie and her boy ran off into the brush and hid out until it was all over. Then, broke and discouraged, Maggie, stuck the boy with relatives and went to work at one of the Dodge City saloons.

Guess the Sheriff there at the time, thought he couldn't prove she was involved as much as her husband was and looked the other way."

"Wasn't long after that the Captain rode through there when the war ended. She made a big fuss over him, him being a big Civil War hero and all, and he decided what his ranch back here needed was a woman's touch."

Maggie looked from one man to another as though trying to see how much they believed of his story.

"My guess is, you never told him you'd been married before. You just high-tailed it out of town as fast as you could so your history wouldn't catch up to you, isn't that right?"

Maggie ignored the Sheriff's question.

"Bet you never told him you had a son, either. Sad thing is, I guess the Captain didn't figure on your greed costing him his life and his ranch — someday."

"You can put your pencil away, son. Looks like Maggie'll be going to jail for a long time, if she doesn't become the first woman to be hung here."

"Hung? You can't hang me, Sheriff, I didn't kill the Captain."

"No, but it isn't hardly fair that your boy gets hung alone when you were the one to hatch the plan. Either way, neither of you will see daylight again, I'm sure."

"You've got no proof, like I said."

"Maybe not on you right this minute. But once your boy, Simmons, finds out he's apt to hang, he may not want to go it alone. Not when it was your idea in the first place.

He's bound to give us a confession to try to save his own skin. Can't say you wouldn't do the same."

"You won't get anything out of the ranch the Captain built up. If he didn't leave a will, and you haven't presented one yet, the State'll claim the land and the buildings as well as the livestock to pay for the expenses of prosecuting the both of you. They'll probably auction it off and, if either of you survive, use the funds to pay for keeping you in whatever prison they decide on. That is, of course, unless they decide you both should hang."

Sheriff Jamison rose to his feet. He reached for the key ring and came around the desk.

"Come on Maggie, you might as well take the cell next to your son. Sure hope he isn't mad enough at you to cause you any harm. If I was you, I'd stay way to the other side of the cell — out of reach. Don't know how it'll go when I have to toss the both of you into the Tumbleweed Wagon and haul you to the County Seat."

Charlie escorted Marguerite Hollingsworth Simmons Collier down the hall and into the vacant cell.

He turned the key in the lock and walked away.

Charlie Jamison returned to his desk and motioned with his hand for the clerk to give him the notes.

He read them over closely, then reached in his desk drawer for his bottle of ink and pen. He removed the glass stopper from the bottle and dipped the nib of the pen into the ink.

Carefully, he signed the last sheet of paper. He pulled a blotter from the drawer and rocked it back and forth across his signature before blowing his breath across the letters to be sure the ink was dry.

The light in the office was dimming as the sky darkened with the threat of another snowstorm blowing in. He lit the lamp and scooted the paper across the desk to Jeremiah sitting in the chair that had so recently held Maggie Collier.

"Sign right below where I did," he told Jeremiah.

Jeremiah hesitated.

"Just make an "X". You can do that, can't you?"

Jeremiah nodded "yes" and looked at the clerk for guidance.

"You best sign that it is his mark and write his name beneath it," Charlie told the clerk.

"Yes, Sir. That's the way we do it at the courthouse."

Charlie felt as if he had just sealed the fates of both Everett Simmons and Maggie Collier.

CHAPTER TWENTY-EIGHT

With Mrs. Collier now in a cell between him and her son, Clay wondered just what had convinced the Sheriff to lock her up. And, why hadn't he set him free when he did? *Did it mean that he would soon be released even though the Sheriff had neglected to do so at the time he brought Mrs. Collier in?* He wanted desperately to know what was going on. He sat on the wooden cot frame wedged into the crevasses of the bricks designed to hold its weight. He leaned his upper back against the wall.

None of the three prisoners spoke.

So, had Mrs. Collier talked with her son when he hadn't been aware of it? Had Simmons been able to overhear the conversation in the outer room?

For now, Mrs. Collier remained silent.

Clay saw her curled up into a ball on the thin mattress pad in her own cell. *No privacy,* he thought.

In the further cell attached to the outside wall, her son tapped his fist on the shutters covering the one cell window that, if it were open, he would only be able to look out through the lattice bars into a narrow alleyway.

209

Surely, Mrs. Collier and her son hadn't named him in their plot! Clay thought with uneasiness.

But it was dark and he was going into another night of confinement. Nightfall meant, as well, perhaps Holly would come in soon with another meal for him. Perhaps she would have gotten some sort of information out of the Sheriff. Or, retained a lawyer for him.

Clay adjusted into a more comfortable position. He tried to call upon his patience to wait for the food he was sure Holly would bring.

After what seemed like an hour he heard the hall door open. Light filtered down the hallway. The keys jingled on the Sheriff's large metal ring as he and Holly walked toward the cell.

When the Sheriff unlocked the cell and pushed the door open he asked, "Would you rather eat here or go on back to the O'Flannery place to eat?"

Clay had already risen to greet Holly but, though they each were still on opposite sides of the bars, they were equally shocked at the Sheriff's comment.

Clay reached back on the bunk for his hat and spun out the cell door before the Sheriff could change his mind.

"Not so quick. Stop by my desk and Jeremiah will give you your personal items."

Holly hurried behind Clay to the desk.

Jeremiah already had what little Clay had carried in his pockets lying on the desk.

Holly was so excited that Clay was free she wore a wide grin and wanted to pound congratulations between his shoulder blades with her fists for want of any other action she might take in public.

"Sheriff, I'll leave the food here. Honora has more ready at home. I'll send someone to pick up the basket and dishes tomorrow morning."

"One thing for sure, we've had plenty to eat while you were a guest here," Charlie told Clay. "Honora is one fine cook. But, I think I'll pass tonight. The Mrs. is expecting me home for dinner." His latter words were directed at Holly.

"Jeremiah can feed the two in the back and himself. I'm sure none of it will go to waste."

"Thank you so much, Sheriff," Holly said. "You're more than welcome to do whatever you want with it. I'm happy to have Clay released."

Clay extended his hand.

"My thanks, too, Sheriff. I assume this means I'm free to go about my life."

"Well, I do need you to stay around until the trial is over. But, you're not under suspicion any more. I'll see that the word is passed. In fact, Silas, down at the paper, will get the whole story once I'm free to tell it."

"I appreciate that. I just want everyone to know my name is still honorable."

"One more thing," the Sheriff said.

A chill ran down Clay's spine.

Oh no, he thought and looked at Holly with worry.

"I thought you might be interested to know that, in due time when the courts find them guilty, and I'm sure they will, the Collier Ranch will most likely be auctioned off."

Visions of the acreage and structures rolled through Clay's mind.

"Just thought you might want to know. If you're tough enough to get past all this, you might be interested in bidding on it."

Clay thought for a bit and looked at Holly.

"I'll give it some consideration, Sheriff," he said, knowing the possibility of purchasing it was out of his grasp. He had very little money in his pants' pocket and none in the bank. Still, there was the promise of the reward money.

~*~

Once out of jail and into the brisk fresh air outside, Clay drew in deep breaths of air that no longer seemed stale and tainted with odors. He took Holly's hand and folded it through the crook he made in his arm and onto his coat sleeve.

Holly looked at him in the dim light cast by windows of nearby buildings.

"I'm sorry I put you to so much trouble," Clay told her.

"It wasn't your fault, Clay," Holly assured him.

"Well, I don't ever want to be in a spot like that again! I do appreciate that you saw that I had excellent meals and did what you could to help."

"There's something I should tell you," Holly hesitated and Clay studied her face with concern.

"Pa came home from Europe early."

Clay absorbed her comment and, knowing Ian O'Flannery, thought that it did not surprise him much. Ian never seemed to do what one expected him to do.

"In that case, I don't think I should go back to your house," Clay said.

"There's nowhere else for you to go! After the hotel burned down the others as well as the boarding houses and spare rooms filled up. The weather's been too bad for the miners to get out into the hills so they've been straggling in since Christmas."

"Just the same, your father has never liked me. And now could be a bad time to show up at his house."

"Clay, he hasn't changed! He'll be in such a drunken state I doubt he will even know you are there."

"I hope you're right. There isn't much chance of finding work around this time of year. And, you heard the Sheriff, I have to stick around until the trial to testify."

"I know. That's why I say we should risk you staying at

our house."

Secretly, following the Sheriff's orders wasn't Clay's only reason to hang around. He had hoped, now that his future looked like it was straightening out, he might be able to include Holly in it.

They entered the house by the kitchen door.

"Mr. Clay, it is so good to see you back," Honora greeted them.

"My father isn't going to like it if he finds out Clay is staying with us, Honora."

"Pshaw!" Honora let out a sound of disgust. "The Mister came down late this evening.

He glanced at the paper and shook it hard before stomping out the door without any breakfast, lunch or dinner. Something in there seemed to upset him more than usual."

Amy and Bradley raced into the kitchen.

"Clay! Clay! Clay is back!" Forgetting to call him Mr. Bingham, they cheered together loud enough anyone within earshot could hear.

"I'd like to get into some clean clothes," Clay excused himself to go up to the room where his belongings had been left while Holly filled Honora in on what had transpired.

When he crossed the threshold between the kitchen and sitting room he stooped to pick up the newspaper that was still spread on the floor.

He couldn't help but wonder what would upset Ian so badly in one of his sober or hung over moments.

Carefully, Clay folded the pages into order and continued across the room and up the stairs.

The room was dark and he could probably have changed his clothes without a problem with the shaft of light that entered from the hall. Instead, he relit the lamp Honora had extinguished earlier and sat on the edge of the bed to unfold the weekly newspaper.

Crimped tightly by Ian's fists earlier, the page listing mining stocks had taken the most damage. It was apparent by the torn paper page that Ian did not like what he saw. The sheet appeared as if he had grasped a hand on each edge and ripped the paper half-way down the page.

Clay studied the report of the fall of stock for gold and silver. The market appeared to be crashing. He wondered if Holly knew. He doubted Ian would have the nerve to tell her. If Ian had ever needed an excuse to drink, he certainly had one now.

Having become accustomed to this new way of life, unless Ian had saved a whole lot of money, which was unlikely, the family was headed for trouble.

From what he knew of Ian O'Flannery, he doubted very much there was sufficient, if any, cash stowed away.

Clay left the paper, folded to the front page, on the bed. He gathered his clothes which appeared to have been recently laundered and stacked nearby. He changed into his newest pants and best shirt to go back downstairs.

CHAPTER TWENTY-NINE

Honora saw that the children were out of the way before Clay and Holly sat down to eat. She set the table in the formal dining room for two with Holly's best china and crystal goblets on a tatted-lace tablecloth. Candles were lit in the center of the table instead of on the overhead chandelier. A low container held a few dried strawflowers from last summer's harvest. Those, Holly had carefully stored with their stems tied together and hung upside down to dry in the pantry. They were as bright as they were at the time they were cut.

"Oh, Honora, how nice!" Holly said as she entered the dining area. "This is very festive. We can celebrate Clay's release and our good fortune to have him back in our lives. Thank you."

"Did I hear the word celebrate?" Clay asked as he entered the room.

"Look. Honora has prepared a delicious meal for us and dressed the table up."

"It looks very nice, Honora," Clay complemented her. Personally, he would have been more comfortable with a plain table where it didn't matter if a spot of gravy dripped off the rim of his plate. He made a note to be especially careful that he didn't stain the luxurious cover or break the fragile-appearing crystal. He had never eaten at such an elegant table in his life. If this was the way Holly liked to live, he wasn't sure he could be comfortable amidst expensive things.

Honora poured a deep red wine into each of their glasses.

"Burgundy," Holly explained. "Simple but it will complement the type of meat Honora is serving. She reached to remove the covers from the serving dishes.

"If you need anything else, Mr. Clay or Miss Holly, just call. I'll be nearby checking on the children or in my room."

"Thank you, Honora," Holly dismissed her. "And thank you for the thoughtful and delightful dinner setting. I'm sure Clay and I will both enjoy it."

As soon as Honora left the room Clay moved his chair and his table setting to where he sat close beside Holly instead of at the opposite end of the table.

"Your hospitality has been outstanding, Holly. And your help with the trouble I was in — I couldn't have been better cared for."

"A toast to all that being behind us," Holly said and raised her glass toward his.

"And to the radiant beauty that sits beside me tonight," Clay added as his eyes took in the glow of candlelight radiating from her face.

She wore a dress as blue as some of the deepest lakes he had seen in the high mountains of Montana. Only an ecru edging outlined her creamy skin above her breasts from the deeper color. A demure diamond necklace sparkled back at him twinkling nearly as brightly as her eyes that seemed to match, or reflect, the tint of the dress.

Holly's face flushed at the complement.

She smiled her most pleasant smile and hid the tears that threatened to well into her pupils and turn them into pools nearly as wet as the Montana lakes.

She knew she had to tell him she must leave for school in only a few more hours. What would she do then? What would Clay do? Would she be gone while he spent his time in court helping to convict the Captain's killer? She knew he had to be there for the trial. She also knew she could not stay.

Holly tilted her head, slightly, to let her hair fall away from her face. She brightened her thoughts and gave Clay a genuine smile. Tomorrow she would worry about all that.

For tonight, it was the most romantic time she had every shared with him and she wanted to savor every minute of the evening. It reminded her of that long-ago Christmas Eve. Nostalgia wafted over her. *But, they were inexperienced, unsophisticated kids then,* she reminded herself.

Clay reached over and laid his hand over hers.

"You are very beautiful, Holly." He lifted her hand and brought her to her feet. Slowly he began to hum a waltz and danced her around the room as though a full orchestra was playing.

Holly threw her head back and laughed.

"Why, Sir, you do flatter me so."

Clay nuzzled his face into her hair near her ear. He released his hand from her back and slowly reached to undo the pins where the cascading curls she had worked so hard to control were gripped to the crown of her head. The silky tresses fell across his fingers of one hand while his other hand guided her. Clay's tune had slowed, as had their movement. They rocked back and forth tight to each other's body simply enjoying the closeness that past circumstances had stolen from them.

"Someday, my love," Clay whispered.

"Someday?" She questioned as she leaned her head back to look into his eyes.

"That's a promise for the future." He knew he could not stay so tight to her body now. He moved slightly away feeling that if he didn't, he might lose control and take her right there in her father's kitchen. He had to wait until there was a way to ask her to marry him before he could partake of her body and she of his.

Clay seated Holly back at the table.

"We best do justice to Honora's fine dinner," he said as he moved back to his own chair.

Languishing informally, they talked of old times and brought each other up to the present with tales of their lives since the last they were together as young adults.

When dessert was over, although they could have talked all night, they let the conversation slow to a pause and prepared themselves to part.

Clay repeated his earlier promise, "Someday." he said. "For now, goodnight." He arose and kissed her gently before turning toward the stairs.

He took the steps quickly leaving both of them to try to fall asleep with their bodies still aching for one another.

CHAPTER THIRTY

The next morning Clay awoke early. He had decided what he would do. Last night had been the most wonderful night of either of their lives and, with the assurance that this mess about the Captain would soon be behind him, he knew the direction of his plan.

He hurried down to breakfast with Holly and the children.

There seemed a more content atmosphere in the home and at the table.

Although they ate in the sunny kitchen area where the room was built to accommodate a smaller, less elegant table, the essence of the previous night still lingered.

Even Bradley and Amy seemed to sense something was different. They both watched their elders as though looking for a sign of what made their world seem brighter.

Bradley whispered to Amy while the two adults talked.

"Why is Holly so happy?"

"I don't know. She's always some happy," Amy answered.

"Not like this. Don't you feel it? I've never seen her act

this way."

"How?"

"She's got on one of her best dresses for breakfast."

"So?" Amy became indignant. "Can't a girl wear what she wants? I will when I grow up."

"You're too little to understand," Bradley gave her a hard look instead of kicking her in the shins like he wanted to.

"Maybe it's because Clay's back," he shrugged and let his concern go. But, Clay and Holly certainly did seem different to him. Too bad if Amy couldn't see it, too. Still, he felt mature and elevated above his sister's level sensing there was something different going on.

When Clay finished his meal, he excused himself and went directly to Holly. He reached for her hand and led her to the entry outside the pantry where they could have a private conversation.

"I have something I need to do. Don't worry. I'll be back shortly." He leaned down and kissed her, first on the forehead and then with a full embrace and a kiss on the mouth.

At first she allowed the kiss but when Clay's mouth found hers, she struggled a bit for fear one of the children would follow them into the ante way. When she relented she found his wanting kiss irresistible and let her body move closer to him until they were meshed together like a married couple.

"Screech," The sound startled both of them.

"Holly, Bradley's getting down without being excused," came Amy's voice.

"Tattle-tale!"

"Well, you are."

Holly and Clay broke apart leaving each other breathless and considering how close they may have come to getting caught in their embrace.

Holly brushed at her hair and, then, the skirt of her dress.

Clay ran his fingers through his own light-brown hair. He reached for his coat on the hook by the back door.

Quickly he kissed Holly's fingers before he broke away.

"I'll be back soon," he said and opened the door to walk the short distance to the business district.

Holly couldn't know where he was going. He would guard his secret until there was reason to tell. The time was not yet.

~*~

Clay began checking each saloon as he came to it. He knew his luck would not be with him in finding Ian sober but he felt he had to try. He wanted the man to know he was being cleared of all charges and hoped Ian would be clear-headed enough to understand.

It was hard to catch him between a hangover and being drunk. And nearly impossible ever to find him stark sober.

Finally, at the Silver Bar Saloon, Clay spotted the man. He leaned back in what appeared to be a drunken stupor in his tilted chair against the wall.

A bottle of whiskey sat on the table in front of him. It was half-full. Knowing Ian, Clay didn't anticipate he would leave the saloon at least until he drained the bottle. He had long since stopped drinking from a shot glass. The one that came with the whiskey lay empty on its side halfway across the table.

"Give me some strong coffee, bartender," Clay said as he pulled a coin from his pocket to pay for it. "Just give me two mugs and the whole pot."

The bartender looked at him as if he were crazy to think he would sober Ian O'Flannery up. Still he stacked one mug inside the other and sat them and the coffeepot on the bar, turning the handles toward Clay.

Clay picked up what he hoped would be a sobering liquid and headed to Ian's table with the coffee and mugs.

He kicked Ian's chair leg when he reached the table.

Ian lunged forward. He squinted his eyes trying to bring Clay's face into focus. Slowly recognition came to his numbed mind.

"What the hell are you doin' here?"

"I came to talk to you. Drink this for awhile until you get some of that fuzz out of your head. Then we'll talk."

"Got nothin' to say to you."

"Drink, anyway. I've got plenty to say to you and I want you're head as clear as it can be to hear it. Now, drink before I pour it down your gullet."

Reluctantly Ian took the filled mug Clay held out to him into his shaking hands.

Clay poured his own coffee and straddled a chair backwards facing the man. He rested his arms across the top of the chair back while he studied Holly's father.

Ian sipped slowly. Every time he looked up at Clay, Clay motioned for him to drink more.

Clay didn't know how long it would take to get him in a sensible condition but he planned to pour coffee as long as it held out. He'd order another pot if need be. Ian was going to listen to what he had to say. And, he was going to do what he could to make him understand.

Once Clay felt Ian might grasp his words, he emptied the dregs of the first pot of coffee into Ian's mug.

"Crap, that's bitter stuff. Full of grounds," Ian sputtered.

"Then chew it. At least it's knocking the edge off your boozed fog." Clay could tell by his complaints that Ian was beginning to think more clearly.

"I'm not here to ask to marry your daughter. I don't need to. We're both old enough, now, to make that decision ourselves. I'm here to tell you that I am going to ask her to marry me."

Ian looked at him with disbelieving eyes. This was something he had protested against ever since Clay came into Holly's life years ago. He didn't object because of the boy himself, then, but because he needed Holly to care for the rest of his children at the time. It was a convenience for him. At first because he could barely feed and house them and still manage to drink. Then, when he became wealthy, he could afford a housekeeper and Holly could go to school to keep her away from rowdy cowboys and lowlife.

Now, as he faced the possibility of, once more, being poor he needed to rethink how he felt about Holly's marrying.

He stared at Clay in silence.

Clay walked to the bar and sat the empty coffeepot on the counter. He motioned to the bartender and received a fresh pot of the steaming brew.

He poured yet another stream of the black liquid into Ian's mug.

"Here, try this," he said. "Maybe it'll wash some of the dregs down your throat and you'll stop complaining. Besides, I'm sure I just gave you something else to complain about. The way I see it, Holly's legal age, now. If she'll have me, I intend to make her my wife."

"What makes you think she'll settle for someone that makes his living as a cowhand? You think she wants to be stuck with someone like that — living hand to mouth instead of all she has now."

Clay didn't answer because it was a question he had asked himself. *Would Holly give up her luxury life to follow him to some ranch somewhere away from all she has come to know?* He had to stand strong with Ian if there was even a chance to find out.

"Like I said. I don't need your permission. We're both legal age. I'll sign an affidavit to that effect so we can get a Marriage License, if I have to."

Ian, anxious to get back to his drinking and knowing the writing on the wall from the newspaper report of the falling stock market, tried to hang tough. He didn't want Clay to think he was giving in too easily. He wouldn't give them his blessing but he now saw their marriage as a way out for himself.

"And where do you think you can do that? The traveling Judge doesn't come to town that often."

"If the Justice of the Peace, here, can't give me the paperwork and sign it, I'll go to the County Seat."

"That's a long ride. Anything could happen to a person alone between here and the County Seat and back."

Clay thought about the threat. He well knew a man could get killed on the road. The Captain had. But, he calculated Ian to be a weak drunk. He probably still had money that could buy a gunslinger, if he wanted. But would he spend it to get rid of him or choose to save it for his future binges? Clay was sure he would choose the latter. Clay tossed that idea aside. Ian knew his good fortune was coming to an end. He was too selfish to spend the money on anything but his next drink. No, Clay didn't believe Ian's threats. Just the same, he would do what he needed to in order to protect himself. Nothing was going to stop him from marrying Holly. Not her father. Not his threats. Nothing.

Although he made it a practice not to wear a gun, if he was forced to ride to the County Seat under these conditions, he would arm himself.

Ian studied him and, even in his semi-sober state, recognized the determined look on Clay's face.

At last he spoke, "I won't give you permission. But, I

won't try to stop you, either."

Clay nodded. "Fair enough! That's all I want. Not that I care what you try to do to me but I don't want any trouble for Holly."

"There's one thing you gotta do. One condition to the deal. You have to take the little kids, too. I don't want to be stuck with them."

Clay wondered how a father could so easily pass his children over to someone else. Especially someone he appeared to have such distaste for. But, he knew, even if Ian didn't, that he would be doing them a favor. He believed they'd be better off somewhere on a ranch or homestead than being in danger in a town. Or, existing with their father. A father who was not likely to change his ways.

"Don't expect anything from me," Ian warned in a gruff voice. He didn't intend to tell anyone that the stocks were falling and he might well lose everything anyhow. Alone he could drink to his heart's content. When the money ran out he could call in some favors and get his alcohol from others he had fronted money and drinks to in the past. He had no doubt he could go back to the way it was in his former life. He had bought a lot of friends drinks while he was riding high. Surely they would return his favors if he was, once again, down and out.

Clay left the coffeepot sitting on the table. He walked away without another word to Ian.

He knew the truth and, even if Ian had wanted to argue, he was no match for Clay.

They both knew it.

When Clay left the saloon behind a young boy rushed toward him.

"Mr. Bingham?" His voice squeaked with the effects of puberty as he spoke toward Clay's back.

Clay turned to see who was calling his name.

He recognized the boy as Sheriff Jamison's nephew.
"What can I do for you?"
"My uncle wants to see you. He sent me to fetch you."
Curiosity jabbed at Clay's mind.
"Did he say what was on his mind?" Clay wondered with a twist in his gut. *Could something have gone wrong? Would he find himself back in jail? Accused again of a crime he didn't do? Should he run?* He decided against that. The Sheriff would merely track him down. Knowing he was in town, it wouldn't take long for him to be found, he judged.

He decided to steel his nerves against the worst possibilities and make his way to the Sheriff's Office.

"Thanks, kid," he told the boy. He stood trying to quiet his breathing and calm his mind as he watched the boy turn and run back down the street toward the Sheriff's home.

Inside his office Sheriff Jamison sat at his desk studying papers spread out before him.

He looked up when Clay entered.

"Howdy, Clay," the Sheriff greeted him without enthusiasm.

Was he in trouble, again?

"Howdy Sheriff. You wanted to see me?"

"Pull up a chair. We've got some business to do."

"What do you mean?" Clay scraped the chairs legs as he sat down and scooted the chair tighter to the Sheriff's desk.

"See all these papers here?"

"Yes." He recognized the log book that he knew carried the Captain's brand on the back cover.

"I took a ride out to the Collier house after we talked about how he branded things — like this book — with that tiny branding iron he had."

Clay watched him pull a single piece of paper from beneath the book.

"Anyway, I found the Captain had a small safe hidden

there under the floor boards in his library. Me and the deputies were finally able to pry it open. Its lucky Maggie didn't find it first. And, it's lucky, for you, we didn't find this paper before we got a confession out of Simmons and Maggie signed her deposition. Not that she really admitted to anything. But she released any claim she had on the Captains estate."

Clay looked at him with raised eyebrows. *What could he be talking about? What could the Captain have had that might change the outcome of his life?* He studied the paper in the Sheriff's hand but could not see the writing with the blank side of the sheet facing him.

"Well, now, if I'd seen this while I had you locked up — this might have capped the possibility of your conviction."

Clay felt an icy stab in his intestines.

"No need to turn so white, Clay. You look like you seen a ghost. You know what this paper is?"

"No! I don't know anything beyond what I told you about the branded cover on some of the Captain's books. The one there on your desk, for example."

"Well, it seems the Captain did leave a Last Will and Testament after all. Guess he wasn't so blind to his wife's crimes like we thought. He may not have ever thought she'd go after him. But, he didn't totally trust her either. So, he left his ranch to you, Clay."

"What? That can't be! We weren't kin. Why would he do that?"

"Here. Read it for yourself. 'Course, I'll have to file it with the court. But, you get it all." The Sheriff handed the yellowed sheet to him.

Clay's hand shook the paper with a rattle as he attempted to read the Captain's handwriting between the vibrations of the inked words on the sheet.

"He did leave some money to his wife and her choice to

stay in the house, if she'd chose to. 'Course you don't have to worry about that now. She'll have a place to stay. Up to the courts. But I'm pretty sure she'll not get out in her lifetime."

Clay felt a rush of excitement trill up into his face where his mouth formed a weak smile.

"I can't believe it." He handed the Will back to the Sheriff.

"Believe it. You must have made the Captain proud."

"Thank you, Sheriff. That means a lot to me."

Clay stood and parted hastily from the Sheriff.

"Don't forget," the Sheriff called after him as he opened the door, "we'll need you at court when it convenes."

Clay raised his hat to let him know he heard. For now, he was too excited to keep the news to himself. He had to rush back to Holly with the good news. On the way he tried to form a plan on how to propose to her when he reached the house.

As he passed the last store, he broke into a run. He wanted to jump and shout and call his good fortune out to the world. But, instead, he tried to hold his joy in until he could share it with Holly.

He heard the train whistle in the distance over the sound of his pounding feet tramping on the boardwalk at the edge of town.

CHAPTER THIRTY-ONE

When Clay reached the gate of the O'Flannery home place, he unlatched it and headed directly for the front door.

Respecting that he was still a guest in the house, he rapped the brass knocker against its heavy brass plate in the shape of a shield attached to the door.

Honora answered the door still wiping her hands on her apron.

Clay grasped the unsuspecting woman by her forearms and danced her into the living area.

"Mr. Clay! Mr. Clay! What are you doing?"

"Honora! I have the best news! Where is Holly? I have to let her know!"

"Mr. Clay, Miss Holly is gone!"

"Gone? Gone where?"

"She had to return to school. She said to tell you she'd be back in the spring."

All Clay's joy sank with his realization he wouldn't see Holly and share the happy news with her. He wouldn't be able to tell her that they were to be married. He wouldn't be able to let her know that they would have a ranch to work that was their own.

He wanted to vocalize his disappointment but feared a loud outburst would frighten Honora and the children.

"Why didn't she tell me?" Was this payback for his leaving without warning in the past? *No, no, he knew Holly better than that. She was not a vengeful person.*

"The children? Where are Amy and Bradley?"

"They were both terribly upset," Honora said. "Miss Amy was crying and crying so badly. Mr. Bradley was kicking his heels and hitting his fists on the floor. To calm them, Miss Holly let them ride with her to the train station. Joshua will bring them back."

"Of course, the train. I heard it whistle when I was on my way here." He was jolted out of his fog of misery.

"Miss Holly left you a note on the dining room table."

"What time does the train leave?" Clay asked as he rushed to the table.

There, leaning against a sugar bowl alongside the silver candlestick bases and dish with its strawflowers was a pale beige piece of paper.

"It is scheduled to leave in a short time."

Clay unfolded the paper. There in a woman's flourished penmanship was his name.

"Dearest Clay," Holly had begun.

Clay read quickly as he made his way back to the front door.

"I am so sorry to have to tell you in this way that I had to catch my train back to school. I didn't want to spoil our evening last night by bringing it up then. I had hoped to relay the problem to you when you returned this morning. But, when you did not arrive in time, I simply had to go or be late returning to classes. That would never do for one who hopes to make a difference in this world for women's futures."

She continued, "Please forgive me. My time with you has been so precious I could not bear to bring this up and spoil our time together. Please keep my love for you in your heart until we can be together again. Yours always, Holly."

Clay was already running before he had the note tucked into his pocket. He had no time to waste. He knew the train would turn around quickly and be headed east in too few minutes. *How long had it been since he heard its first whistle?* He couldn't gauge. He only knew, he must — not — miss — it!

His heart was pounding faster than his feet could go.

Ahead he could see the smoke emitted from the train's smokestack lifting into the air above the depot's roof. If the train left the platform before he got there, he'd be unable to catch it and Holly would be gone.

He felt his heart skip a beat and wasn't sure if the ache he felt there was from the effort he was putting out racing for the train station or from the fact that he was, perhaps, seconds away from losing Holly.

Who knew what would happen if she got back to Boston. Perhaps a young rich fellow classmate would woo her and win her heart. Maybe she would decide not to return in the spring.

He thought all sorts of dark thoughts as he leaped onto the platform next to the rail where the train sat.

He saw Joshua, Amy and Bradley standing on the walkway staring at the window of a passenger car.

"All aboooooooard!" The Conductor called.

Clay bounded past the startled families waving goodbye to their loved ones.

The Conductor reached to pick up the step stool that allowed passengers to climb to the first step of the train. Clay's foot hit it firmly, dropping it back to the platform as he sprinted onto the passenger coach.

Inside he walked quickly down the aisle looking for the familiar face of his own loved one.

Holly, where are you? His eyes searched each seat. He glanced over his shoulder and saw the Conductor following him.

At last, a young woman who had been bending over behind a seatback rearranging her carpetbag straightened up.

"Holly!"

"Clay!" She said in surprise.

He reached her with the Conductor only a few rows of seats behind him.

"I thought I wouldn't get to say goodbye — " Holly began.

The Conductor grasped Clay's arm.

"Sir! You must get off so I can signal the Engineer to leave," he tugged at Clay.

"Give me just a few minutes, please."

"No, Sir. I can't. You are delaying our departure. You will throw us off schedule."

Clay jerked his arm free and dropped to his knees besides Holly.

"Holly, don't go. I have wonderful news!"

"Clay, I don't want to go. But, I have a commitment to return to school, What can I do?"

She looked at him with tears in her eyes as she fretted. She glanced outside the window where she saw the two children. Tears streamed down Amy's face and Bradley rubbed one eye and then the other as he tried to hide the fact that he, too, was crying.

She looked into Clay's pleading eyes.

"Sir! Do I have to get help to get you off the train so we can leave?"

Clay ignored the man and addressed Holly.

"Holly, I love you. Will you marry me? I promise you, I can provide for you — and the children. Captain Collier left me his ranch in his Will. We can share the work and the profits. I promise you, we will be equal partners in whatever we do."

Holly gasped.

The Conductor moved away to go for help.

Clay knew he had very little time left before he would be dragged off the train and, perhaps, housed back in Sheriff Jamison's jail.

"I know you may not want to live in the old ranch house with so many bad memories that have been left there. But, I know that land so well, I know where there's a beautiful meadow with a slight rising hill that we can build a house on. A home just for us and the kids and the babies we'll have of our own."

"Oh, Clay! Yes! I have been waiting for you to ask me to marry you ever since you returned!"

Clay rose to his feet tugging Holly to a standing position as well.

Despite a crowded passenger car containing men, women and children, he drew her to him and kissed her firmly.

Women passengers covered the eyes of their children with their hands. Others gasped behind their handkerchiefs. The men hooted and called out brash comments. Some of the children giggled at this display they were privy to for the first time in their lives.

"There will be this and much more to come," he whispered in her ear. "For now, we need to get out of here before that Conductor comes back and has us both jailed."

"But, my luggage," Holly protested as they moved apart and Clay led her by her hand toward the door.

"We'll have it picked up at the other end and shipped

back. Thank goodness for the telegraph. We can let the clerk at the other end know we need it returned."

When they reached the opening to leave the train Holly hesitated and thought of her earlier goals in life.

Should she have said "yes" to Clay so quickly and miss out on becoming an attorney? Changing her part of the world? His proposal, once it happened, seemed to have started her thoughts spinning at a rapid speed. All of it was coming at her too fast.

They both saw the Conductor moving down the aisle with Deputy Jeremiah beside him.

Still Holly didn't step down from the train car.

She turned to Clay. "I'd rather be a rancher's wife than a rich spinster. But, I want you to promise me, if I marry you, no matter how long it takes I can still become a lawyer. That you won't get upset if I work for women's rights to vote and to own their own property instead of having to let their husbands control their assets only in his name."

She looked back at Jeremiah and the Conductor closing in fast. Then, turned her attention quickly to Clay standing on the platform waiting for her to put her foot on the stepstool and come into his arms.

Clay grinned as he listened to Holly say her piece.

"I wouldn't even try to stop you, if I could. Why, you already sound like you've written your Dissertation."

He held both hands in the air.

"You win, My Love. In fact, legal or not we'll put your name on the deed to the Circle 2 C and rename the Ranch. We'll figure out a brand and you can file it. Now, let's get out of here before we both get arrested and you have to lawyer us out of jail."

Clay helped Holly to the platform and they stepped far enough away to let the Conductor pick up his stepstool.

Holly put her arms around Clay's neck and kissed him as

the train began to chug slowly away from the station.

She removed her lips from his long enough to say, "Yes. I love you Clay Bingham."

"I love you, too, Holly O'Flannery — soon to be Bingham." He grinned.

Steam and coal smoke from the train engine drifted back to them as Amy and Bradley rushed forward to clutch the couple around their legs and join in their embrace. Amy wrapped her arms as high as she could and Bradley held tight to his taller grasp.

"Does this mean you aren't going back to school?" Bradley asked Holly.

"Not for awhile. And, when I do, Clay will be home with the both of you.

"We're all going to be a family, now," Clay assured the children.

Immediately they ran to Joshua with the good news.

The End

ABOUT THE AUTHOR

Mary Jean Kelso is a multi-genre author. Her children's books include a dozen or more titles. She is, also, the author of four young adult novels and several adult novels. Her only factual book is a genealogy title about her lineage down from her great-great grandfather, who was killed at the Alamo, **A Visual History Record of Alamo Defender Gordon Cartwright Jennings' Family** (co-authored with her daughter, **Wendy Whiteman**).

Many of her children's books are available in Braille through Xavier Society for the Blind (http://xaviersociety.org/) and The Anna B. Repicky Foundation (http://www.annabfoundation.org/).

Mary Jean contributes to Local and National newspapers and magazines and was an Asst. Editor prior to concentrating on fiction. She has received awards from The National Press Assn. and The Nevada Press Assn. She is a member of The Daughters of the American Revolution, The Alamo Defenders Descendants Association, The Daughters of the Republic of Texas, The Alamo Society and Made in Nevada — www.madeinnevada.org.

Visit Mary Jean on the Web at :
http://www.maryjeankelsoauthor.wix.com/mjkel

BOOKS BY MARY JEAN KELSO

THE HOMESTEADER
THE HOMESTEADER'S LEGECY
BACK TO THE HOMESTEAD
LIFE ON THE HOMESTEAD
ANNABEL'S STORY
GOODBYE IS FOREVER
NO TIME FOR GOODBYE
NEVER SAY GOODBYE
BLUE COAT
KAT'S CRADLE
THE CHRISTMAS ANGEL
ONE FAMILY'S CHRISTMAS
COWBOY JAMES
RV MOUSE
BIRDS IN THE FLOWER BASKET
ANDY AND THE ALBINO HORSE
ANDY AND SPIRIT GO TO THE FAIR
ANDY AND SPIRIT IN THE BIG RESCUE
ANDY AND SPIRIT MEET THE RODEO QUEEN
ANDY AND SPIRIT IN SEARCH AND RESCUE
THE ADVENTURES OF ANDY AND SPIRIT - BOOK 1
LITTLE LONNIE LONG EARS
A VISUAL HISTORY RECORD OF ALAMO DEFENDER
GORDON CARTWRIGHT JENNINGS' FAMILY